Valentine
VOTE

Susan Blexrud

Author of *His Fantasy Maid* and *The Gettysburg Vampire*

CRIMSON
ROMANCE

F+W Media, Inc.

Published by
Crimson Romance
an imprint of F+W Media, Inc.
10151 Carver Road, Suite 200
Blue Ash, OH 45242. U.S.A.
www.crimsonromance.com

ISBN 10: 1-4405-8011-1
ISBN 13: 978-1-4405-8011-6
eISBN 10: 1-4405-8012-X
eISBN 13: 978-1-4405-8012-3

Cover art © istock.com/keithpix; istock.com/sbayram; istock.com/GlobalStock

Acknowledgments

As always, heartfelt gratitude goes to my incredible critique group, the Pink Fire Writers. Without the weekly input of Jeanne Charters, Beth Robrecht, and Sallie Bissell, my work would consist of a jumble of words in search of meaning.

Also, sincere thanks to the team at Crimson Romance and particularly to Tara Gelsomino, who elevated my little story to a whole new level.

Chapter One

Courtney Larson flipped up the collar on her boiled wool coat, bracing herself for one of the coldest days in a brutal winter. She pushed open the door of the townhouse she shared in Foggy Bottom and squinted into the clear January sky. For a Florida girl, the weather in D.C. had been a rude awakening when she moved to the big city for law school at Georgetown University, but she loved every minute of it. Even the occasional exploding manhole cover in her neighborhood added excitement to the beat of a city that thrived on political tensions and monumental decisions. And being in the thick of it was part of the appeal.

A chilling breeze lifted Courtney's shoulder-length hair out of her coat collar. Strawberry-blonde strands swirled around her face, sticking like fly paper to her raspberry lip gloss. Spitting wisps out of her mouth, she squared her shoulders to the wind, gritted her teeth, and ran the three blocks to her firm.

"Morning," Courtney said to the receptionist, Elise, who jumped out of her chair, almost strangling herself with her headset.

"Mr. Champion wants you in the conference room." Elise pointed down the opposite hall from Courtney's office.

She smiled at Elise and then hurried to her office to deposit her coat and grab her iPad. Courtney assumed Mr. Champion wanted to talk about the tobacco vote and pressed a hand to her fluttering stomach. Everything she'd worked for over the last few years hung on this campaign.

Since her first year in law school, she'd positioned herself for a career in the political arena. As editor of the law review, she'd interned in Congress and then landed her dream job at Montgomery, Haskins & Knoll, one of the most prestigious lobbying firms in the nation's capital. The icing on her professional cake was her first client, the Campaign for Tobacco-Free Kids. It was a major responsibility for a twenty-seven-year-old attorney, fresh out of law school, but her volunteer work had always been in support of non-profits, and she was thrilled that her firm had entrusted her with this challenge. She had until February 14, Valentine's Day, to convince legislators to pass a bill for higher taxes on cigarettes, or as Courtney referred to them, cancer sticks.

This was more than dogged determination on her part; this was a personal vendetta. Her mother, Sylvia, a lifelong smoker, had died of lung cancer. While she'd tried to quit numerous times over the years, the addiction to nicotine always won out. Through six months of chemotherapy, Courtney watched her mom briefly rally and then succumb after a horrible few days of gasping for breath. She'd taken a sabbatical from school and was glad to have been there at the end, but the imprint of Sylvia's death rattle would haunt her forever. Courtney blamed the tobacco companies, with their advertising targeted to young women. What had been promised to make her mother "mysterious and enchanting" ended up killing her. Though it had been more than two years, the pain of her passing still brought a lump to Courtney's throat ... every day. If her efforts could keep one teenager from smoking, her mom would smile down from heaven, and Courtney would know that another family wouldn't experience the horror and pain her own family had endured.

• • •

Opening the door to the conference room, Courtney was surprised to find not only Bill Champion, her immediate boss, but also Alan Montgomery, one of the firm's principals. Bill, always the height of fashion, wore pin-striped Armani, while the erudite Alan wore his signature tweed jacket with elbow patches. Her heart raced. If Montgomery was here, this was more than just a status meeting.

"Miss Larson, don't you look rosy this morning." Alan Montgomery was old school. No one under sixty would make that kind of comment for fear of being hit with a sexual harassment suit. "And we'll need you rosy. Actually, we'll need you marathon ready. How's tobacco doing?"

"Quite good, sir. We've got our votes in the House. I just need to shore up a few senators. If I can convince the one senator from North Carolina with Big Tobacco in his pocket, I feel sure the remaining four votes will be ours."

"And there's the rub," Alan said. Senator Eric Morrison will be a tough nut to crack. His mother's a Roark, the family that brought us the world's best-selling cigarette."

"Yes, sir, but I've been working on an angle." Courtney took a chair at the conference table, joining the two men. She opened her iPad and accessed the campaign's file. She'd created folders for each of the legislators she'd been hired to sway, or rather, *educate*. Delving into their personal lives to find their soft spots, like kids and pets (a dog could even get asthma from secondhand smoke), she'd also identified the friends and family members each legislator could lose as a result of cancer, emphysema and heart disease— all tobacco related conditions. In addition to their familial status, she'd listed everything from hobbies to philanthropic pursuits.

Courtney clicked on the Senator Eric Morrison file. Up popped his gorgeous face—the chiseled jaw, full lips, aquiline nose, and deep-set eyes. She took a few moments to drink in the senator's image, and then realized her superiors were waiting for her. She cleared her throat. "Here's our guy."

"Give me the lowdown," Alan said.

"Never been married, but he's not gay, or at least if he is, he hides it well. Graduated from Yale Law School. He was in a relationship with a woman he met there, but she took a job in

L.A., and they evidently had a parting of the ways because, as far as I can tell, they're not tearing up the airways to see each other. He rarely frequents bars and isn't known as a partier, unless there's a congressional event or fundraiser, in which case he usually makes an appearance, but he doesn't linger. He's known as a moderate Democrat, so at least he's more open-minded than some of the 'no tax' Republicans.

"But anyway, that's all minor stuff compared to the big kahuna. As you know, his contributions from Big Tobacco are substantial. He's surely dug in, but I've got some thoughts for an approach."

Courtney took a deep breath.

"Well, don't keep us in suspense," Bill said. "His background makes him a particularly valuable vote. If someone with a vested interest in tobacco can see the light ... "

"Okay." Courtney fingered her pearl choker. "Well, the last thing he'll want is to be perceived as pandering to the tobacco industry. It would be a major conflict of interest. So we can argue that if he supported higher taxes on tobacco, his political capital would glow with integrity."

"Except that his constituents are from tobacco country, and those folks smoke. If I'm not mistaken, they still smoke in bars in Winston-Salem." Bill nodded. "Check that, will you?"

"Yes sir, I will." Courtney made a note in her iPad. "I'm meeting with Senator Morrison tomorrow, so I'll do reconnaissance today."

"What does he care about?" Alan asked. "Are there any issues he'd trade his tobacco vote for?"

Courtney scanned the Morrison folder. "He's a Big Brother to a foster kid in McLean. He takes the boy to Redskins and Wizards games. There's a photo here of them together at Busch Gardens in Williamsburg." She had to smile at the adorable image of the regal senator and a young boy holding a huge cone of cotton candy. She turned her iPad around so Bill and Alan could see. "And he's spearheaded some efforts for Special Olympics. That's a possibility. There's funding for Special Olympics bundled into a non-profit bill coming up on the floor."

"See if you can work that," Bill said. "Anything else?"

"He's been a spokesman for animal rights, especially for farm animals. He marshaled a bill last year for humane slaughtering." Courtney grimaced. "Isn't that an oxymoron?"

Bill ignored her rhetorical question. He rubbed his chin. "The fellow's a saint."

Courtney wrinkled her nose. "But is he a good guy or is it all for show? I mean, really, can he be that honorable if he endorses tobacco?" She shut her iPad, and then patted it with conviction. "Gentlemen, I want you to know that I won't be happy with anything less than complete satisfaction, and that means Senator Morrison in our camp." She rose from her chair, tucked her iPad under her arm, and strode from the room.

Chapter Two

In law school, Courtney had reeked geek. From her thick eye-glasses to her flat loafers, she exuded the musty fragrance of old books. Anyone that nerdy had to be at the top of the class. And she was.

Of course, part of the reason she'd been such an exemplary student was her lack of distractions. Who needed men when you could get yourself off more quickly and efficiently than any man could? At least any man Courtney had ever met. She was the only post-law school virgin she knew, but she didn't regret the time she'd spent on her studies instead of fawning over a boy. She'd briefly dated a professor at Georgetown, but when he'd started hinting at taking it to the "next level," Courtney had broken it off. Besides, her career was too important to have her grades called into question if it ever came to light.

Later, she had wondered if part of the professor's appeal was his being off limits. Did she like that they had to sneak around because of his status as a professor? Maybe. Could it be that she was still a virgin because she was afraid of love? Would all she'd worked for take a backseat to a man in her life? And would sex addle her brain? She didn't know.

These were questions that had never concerned the old, nerdy Courtney. But since her graduation last June, her roommate, Helen, who was a public defender, had spent an inordinate amount of time on trying to improve Courtney's image. While she still wore her thick eyeglasses at home, Helen made her spring for contact lenses for work. She'd spritzed her with *J'adore* cologne on a trip to Macy's, and then made her buy it. She'd shortened her skirts four inches and made sure her slacks hugged her bum. She'd gifted her with textured tights (her one monetary contribution) and insisted she trade her loafers for pumps and ankle boots that added a few inches to her five foot five frame.

"Your legs and eyes are your 'to die for' features," Helen insisted. "Show them off."

Courtney had spent her first month of work blinking incessantly and pulling her skirts down to cover her knees, but she'd gotten used to her new look. The nods and smiles of appreciation from the opposite sex were novel, but quite nice.

And today's outfit for her meeting with Eric Morrison would say, "Yes, I'm professional, but underneath I'm all woman." The new, hot red lingerie that lurked beneath her business suit would hopefully pump up her power. In law school, her most provocative move was pushing her glasses up the bridge of her nose. Now, with Helen's help, she understood the advantage of using her beauty as well as her smarts. It could be the difference between success and failure for the upcoming vote.

By the time Courtney arrived for her two o'clock appointment at the Hart Senate Office Building, she was already fifteen minutes late. She'd been so engrossed in her research on Senator Morrison that she'd lost track of time and then an exploded manhole cover had forced the taxi to take a long detour. As a result, she knew more about Eric Morrison than was necessary ... or healthy. She was developing a crush, and she hadn't even met him. He was one of those guys who did everything well. She'd seen photos of him horseback riding (he'd won junior championships in dressage), water skiing, snowboarding, pole vaulting (how does *anyone* do that?), and sailing in the America's Cup. The sailing photo looked straight out of a Ralph Lauren ad. It was a close-hauled shot with sails pulled in, and the good senator smiled broadly as he leaned against the rigging. He even had a dimple. Courtney hoped there was just one dimple. Two would just be too ... perfect.

But his voting record wasn't perfect or predictable. In fact, it was an enigma. He'd voted in favor of the smoking ban in restaurants and bars across North Carolina, but he'd voted against the last tax increase on cigarettes. What was up with that?

She checked her coat at the reception desk and passed through the atrium where Alexander Calder's "Mountains and Clouds," one of the sculptor's last works, rose majestically. Courtney would have liked to spend a few moments gazing at it, but she was already late. No time for lollygagging. She took the elevator to the fifth floor.

The senator's office was at the end of a long hall, studded with photos of notables, but again, she couldn't delay. She took a deep breath. The air was heavy with tweed and musty books, just the kind of aroma you'd expect in a contemplative environment. It reminded her of the Georgetown law library. She tugged at the hem of her fitted jacket. Helen had chosen the color, deep purple. She said it enhanced Courtney's blue eyes. She pressed her lips together and then used her pinky to swipe at the space between her cupid's bow where lipstick tended to clump.

She opened the door to face a secretary who looked like she could have worked for J. Edgar Hoover. Not that the woman was that elderly, but her style was definitely from a bygone era. Her eyeglasses swung from a chain around her neck, and she had a pencil stuck in her gray-streaked chignon. "May I help you?" She put on her wire-rimmed glasses and promptly glared over the top of them.

"Yes, thank you. I'm Courtney Larson from Montgomery, Haskins & Knoll. I have a two o'clock appointment with Senator Morrison." Courtney smiled.

"Well, you're late." She frowned. "Won't you have a seat?" Lorena Eddington (Courtney read the nameplate on her desk) buzzed her boss from her desk phone then pointed to the door when a deep voice on the other end said, "Send her in, but I've only got a few minutes."

Courtney had barely taken her seat, and now her knees wobbled as she got up. Must be the new boots. When she pushed open the massive wood door leading to the senator's inner office, he rose from behind his desk and rounded it to greet her. Proffering a hand, she slipped hers into his and looked up into green eyes flecked with gold. Criminy, he was gorgeous. And he was wearing Burberry cologne. She'd given the fragrance to her brother last Christmas, but Senator Morrison didn't look like her goofy brother. Oh, no, the senator was Bradley Cooper with a splash of Michael Fassbender in the set of his strong jaw. Yum.

"Good afternoon, Senator Morrison. I'm Courtney Larson from Montgomery, Haskins & Knoll." Were her hands sweating?

"I see you found your way, finally. I must say that lobbyists are generally punctual. It must have something to do with their intent?" His eyebrows rose with the question, but she didn't miss that his eyes then traveled up and down her body.

"It's inexcusable, but I hope you'll grant me just a few minutes of your valuable time." She didn't wait for him to offer her a chair. She sat, crossed her legs, set her briefcase next to the chair, and ran her fingers up her calf before returning to his gaze. "I'm really sorry I was delayed because what I want to talk with you about is one of the most important issues you'll decide this year. But I can be brief, and I hope, convincing." She smiled.

"Brief away." Senator Morrison sat on the edge of his desk, spreading his long legs out and bracing his hands on either side of his hips. Just the kind of casual, but intimidating, posture she'd expect from him.

"Your voting record would indicate that you care deeply about your constituents. You consistently support bills on education and the environment. In fact, you voted for the ban on smoking in North Carolina restaurants and bars, proving that the health of your citizens is foremost in your mind." Courtney clasped her hands together and leaned forward in her chair. "I know you voted against the last tax increase on tobacco in 2008, but the bill that will come up next month to increase the surcharge by another paltry few cents will help your state fund educational improvements, specifically new programs in the community college system in fields like medicine and engineering." Courtney took a breath, and was getting ready for the rest of her spiel, when Senator Morrison held up a hand to interrupt.

"Pardon me, Miss ... Larson, was it?"

Courtney nodded.

The senator crossed his arms. Someone, like his public relations person, should tell him not to do that. It looked confrontational. "Before you go any further, Miss Larson, I'd like to tell you what I'm doing for my state in the realm of tobacco. I'm pushing the USDA to help tobacco farmers by making an adjustment to the tobacco federal crop insurance program so that claim amounts can better reflect market prices. I'm working on the price election issue in direct response to requests from tobacco farmers all across eastern North Carolina who contacted my office seeking assistance. So far, no one in my district seems to be concerned with teenage smoking."

Courtney straightened in her chair. "While I appreciate your focus on protecting small business owners, have you considered helping farmers transition out of tobacco to a more environmentally-friendly crop ... like hemp? And unlike tobacco, which is harmful in every form, hemp has a multitude of practical uses. I even have a pair of hemp shoes."

Courtney watched the senator's eyes move to her feet, travel slowly up her legs, pause briefly at her calves, and then settle back on her face. She thought she detected a hint of appreciation in his gaze.

"Miss Larson, what you're suggesting is akin to asking Ford to start making Toyotas. You don't just yank out one crop and start planting another. I have to help my farmers where they are in this lifetime ... with the crop that's been on their land for generations."

"What about sustainability, Senator? Looking ahead twenty years and more, wouldn't you want to be supporting a crop that could enhance the planet, rather than one that destroys it?" *Was it getting warm in here?* Courtney fidgeted with her thin gold necklace.

"Just so I understand, you came here to try to convince me of something, and now you're questioning my judgment?" The corner of his mouth twitched. Was he suppressing a scowl or a grin?

He's right. What am I doing? Cool down, Court. "Look, what you're doing with price election is admirable, but it doesn't begin to touch on the crux of the tobacco issue."

"Which is?"

Like he doesn't know. "Which is the recent upswing in tobacco use by teenagers."

"I'm assuming you have statistics on that."

"Absolutely." Courtney reached into her briefcase and pulled out a folder. "I've prepared a dossier of information that you are welcome to use to build your case in the Senate." She handed the folder to Senator Morrison. "I'd be happy to send you electronic copies, as well."

"That won't be necessary at this point," Senator Morrison said. He flung the folder into his desktop inbox, which was already overflowing. "It's important that you know why I took this job, Miss Larson. I work on behalf of the citizens of my district, and the bills I push are ones that I know will directly benefit them."

"Perhaps they don't feel it would be in their best interests to curb teenage smoking. Maybe they'd rather deal with the heartache of lung cancer when those teenagers hit their fifties." Courtney didn't need a cigarette to generate smoke. It rose from her ears and swirled around her head. "As their senator, it's your responsibility to ensure that the future generation is smoke free, and that begins with your constituents. They look to you to lead them, and this is an issue where you can take a noble stand for their health. You say you want to help tobacco farmers, but what help can you be when you're perpetuating the problem?" Add flaring nostrils to those smoking ears.

"Whoa, can we dial it back a bit here?" The senator made the timeout sign, and again, that little mouth twitch seemed to suppress a grin.

"Sorry. Perhaps I got a bit carried away. I didn't mean to tell you how to do your job." She was just trying to appeal to his better nature ... if he had one.

"Didn't you?" He chuckled, displaying that one dimple. "You told me exactly how you think I should do my job."

"I try to remain objective about the issues I represent, but this one is personal. My mother died of lung cancer." She'd had no intention of telling Senator Morrison about her mother, but she didn't want him to think she blathered like that on a regular basis.

"I understand." He spoke slowly, his voice evoking empathy. "Being passionate about an issue is admirable." He looked at her from under his eyelashes. He was either sincere or very good at rhetoric. He checked his watch. She'd vote for the rhetoric. "Listen, you've made a cogent argument, but I'm firm on my position. And right now, I have another appointment. In fact, they're probably waiting."

Courtney's heart sunk to the soles of her black pumps. She couldn't let this defeat her. Think ... think ... think. "Certainly, Senator. I won't take up more of your time, but I'd like to leave you with this passing thought. I know you're a supporter of the Big Brother Program, and I wonder how you'd feel about your little brother, I believe his name is Travis, taking up smoking?"

The senator's eyes grew wide. "I see you've done your research, Miss Larson, and the answer is no, I wouldn't want Travis to start smoking."

"I suspected as much," Courtney said. She wanted to say something about how her information had hit home, but she bit her tongue. Better to let him mull this over.

He nodded, a small smile tugging at his lips. "Can we continue this discussion another time?"

"Certainly. I'll check your schedule on my way out." Courtney bolted up from her chair, and then pressed her fingers to her temple, feeling a bit light-headed.

He opened his mouth, closed it, and then said, "Are you free for dinner tonight, say seven o'clock?"

Mixing business and pleasure—never a good idea. She felt her cheeks blaze. Her mind scrambled for a plausible excuse, but nothing surfaced. *Oh, what the heck. Live a little dangerously, Court.* "Uh, yes I am."

"Great. Leave your address with my secretary."

Minor victory but Courtney would take it. She took a deep breath, finally able to relax, and suddenly her head grew light, her vision blurring—*should've grabbed lunch*—and she blinked hard to focus. There was a collection of photos on the wall behind the senator's desk and Courtney stared hard, willing the brief detached sensation to pass. They were duplicates of the photos she'd seen online: group shots featuring Eric and friends fishing at a lake, posing with horses in equestrian gear, and bundled up on a snowy ski slope. Next to the photos was a framed riding crop. Curious. Something about it spiked her interest. "Do you use that for riding?"

The senator smiled, but this time his lips didn't turn up in a politician's grin or a condescending smirk. This time, his lips curled seductively. "Yes, for all sorts of riding. I have quite a collection at home."

Besides horses, what would he be riding? Oh ... *Don't blush, don't blush, don't blush,* Courtney chanted to herself. And what else might he have in his collection? "I'll ... be ... going ... now."

As she walked away from the senator, she realized she was leading with her neck, which jutted out like a horse just sprung from the paddock, anxious to hit the meadow.

Chapter Three

Courtney had never, ever succumbed to an invitation like the one she accepted from Senator Morrison. And she'd been asked many times, though most of the legislators she met had wives in their home states and were just trolling for some action while they were in session. This time, the legislator was not only unattached, he was drop dead gorgeous.

Well, no time like the present to start thinking about all the reasons she shouldn't be doing this. She was reminded of the movie, *The American President,* with Annette Benning and Michael Douglas. Mr. Douglas played the president, and Ms. Benning was a lobbyist. They got into some sticky situations, including criticism from the president's opponent, citing a conflict of interest. With the tobacco vote looming on the horizon, Courtney dating Senator Morrison would be the Wikipedia definition of conflict of interest.

And then there was the little issue about dating in general. Did she have time for this?

Oh, lighten up, Court. It's one little date, hardly something to cream one's panties over, as Helen would say.

Courtney jumped when the doorbell rang. She'd been trying to keep herself busy by reading the latest issue of Martha Stewart's *Simple Living* magazine, but all that registered in the recipe for Brunswick Stew was that there was no Brunswick in it.

"You look ... lovely."

The senator's eyes traveled from Courtney's freshly bobbed hair to pause at her cleavage (*thank you, black wrap dress*), and then graze across the above-knee hem to end at her leopard pumps. He returned to her eyes, a sheepish grin on his adorable mug.

Courtney smiled. "Would you like to come in for a drink? It's freezing out there."

"Thanks, but I left the car running." He shrugged, perhaps disappointed.

Courtney grabbed her coat out of the hall closet. Eric helped her put it on, briefly brushing her shoulders in the process. Courtney wanted to lean into him. She'd inhaled the briefest hint of his tweedy maleness, laced with Burberry, when he stepped over the threshold. So, instead of rubbing against him (no, she wouldn't actually do that, though it was tempting), she grabbed her clutch bag from the entry table and stuffed her hands into her gloves.

As they rushed to the car, the senator's hand rested on her back, and he opened the passenger door for her. Once he settled behind the wheel, Courtney asked, "Where to?"

"I thought we'd try Zaytinya. Do you like Turkish food?"

"I love it." She'd never tried it. Why did she say she loved it? What was wrong with her? "Actually, I'm not sure I've ever had it." Honesty is always, well, sometimes, the best policy. "Lots of curry, right?"

"It's a lot like Greek food. So, if you like lamb, eggplant, and chicken, you'll be able to find something on the menu. And then there's always octopus."

"I'll bet you didn't grow up on octopus in North Carolina."

He laughed. "Not even close. It was all barbecue, grits, and buttermilk biscuits."

"Followed by chewing tobacco?"

They reached a stoplight, and he took his eyes off the road, turning to her. "Don't tell me you're launching into business already."

"Sorry. I can be kind of intense when I'm involved in something."

"I promise there will be time for your tobacco spiel, but for now, I'd just like to get to know you better." The light changed, and Eric adjusted his rear view mirror before taking off. Courtney looked at his long fingers as they moved the mirror a degree down. She imagined those fingers on her and shifted on the plush leather seat of Eric's Cadillac.

"I'm glad you drive an American car," she said, returning to more practical matters.

"Thanks. I fought for the auto stimulus money, and I'm proud of the turnaround in the industry."

She knew that. She knew everything about his voting record. What she didn't know were his motives. Was it all about his constituents, or did political aspirations rule his decisions?

"Come on, tell me about Washington's up-and-coming lobbyist." He glanced at her from under his eyelashes. "That would be you."

"It's a standard tale." She shrugged. "Geeky bookworm gets scholarship to major law school and lands her dream job."

"No, I mean about what makes you tick. I already know the basics. I Googled you."

"Bet you don't know as much about me as I know about you," Courtney said. "Lobbyists are skilled at digging up dirt."

He half-frowned. "Wait a minute, what kind of dirt are you talking about?"

"Feeling guilty?" Courtney smiled. She gave a dismissive wave. "Let's just say that in reviewing your voting record, I think you're walking a tightrope with your stance on tobacco. You voted for the ban on smoking in restaurants and bars in North Carolina but against the 2008 tobacco tax increase. You're going to be viewed as wishy-washy if you don't watch yourself."

"I study the issues carefully, and I always vote in the best interests of my constituents. You could never fault me on that."

"Really? Even when their health is at stake?" Warmth crept up her neck, and it wasn't from the Cadillac's heated seats.

"Whoa, hold on. Sure you're not a litigator?"

Courtney realized she was coming on too strong. "Sorry. I don't know what's gotten into me. I have this overwhelming urge to make you see the light." Really, why did she care so much? He was just one vote, albeit a significant one. Couldn't she just relax and have a good time with this yummy man?

"You wouldn't be the first woman who wanted me to see the light." One side of his mouth turned up in a grin. Sexy.

I am so sure. "Ha, ha. Don't worry. People don't change unless they want to, and I have a strong suspicion you don't want to."

"True, but *I* have a strong suspicion you like a challenge."

"In my professional life, yes. In my personal life, not so much."

"Have you had many serious relationships, Courtney?"

I guess I asked for that. Ordinarily, she'd consider a man quite brazen for posing such a personal question, especially someone she'd only known for a day, but she was the one who brought up her personal life. Had she invited his question? She felt like she was in the confessional, and Eric was the obliging young priest behind the screen. And she wasn't even Catholic. "Honestly, I've never had what most people would define as 'a relationship' with a man." She couldn't help but use air quotes.

"Does that mean you like women?" He could have been asking whether she liked oatmeal because his expression remained neutral, eyes on the road.

"No, my girlfriends are important to me, but I don't have sex with them." She was surely crimson by now. She turned her head to the passenger window and tried to fan her face surreptitiously.

"So, no steadies even in high school?" He touched her gloved hand, causing her to jump.

Good grief, here we go. Say ten 'Hail Marys' and call me in the morning. "Where are you going with this line of questioning, counsellor? If you must know, I was a total geek in high school and college, and then when I got to law school, I delved even deeper into the books. Now I'm trying to establish a career. It's not like I've been twiddling my thumbs, waiting for Mr. Wonderful to come along."

"Sorry. I hadn't planned to launch into an examination of your romantic history." He tipped his head and glanced at her under his thick eyelashes. "But since we're on the subject, I might as well get this out in the open ... are you a—?"

This is nothing to be ashamed of, so why am I hot under the collar? "Yes, I am a virgin." *Oops, I said that a bit too loudly.*

Eric laughed. "I was going to ask if you were available."

Their conversation was cut short with a turn into the restaurant's valet circle. The attendant opened the passenger door, helping Courtney out, and then he zipped around the car to accept the keys from Eric and drive the Cadillac off to parts unknown.

In the space of about ten minutes, Courtney had revealed more about herself than some of her best friends knew. She needed to tone it down. More importantly, she had to convince this enigmatic man that she was right about a higher tax on tobacco. She figured she had about two hours to set him straight. And considering how things were proceeding so far, it wouldn't be easy.

• • •

They were both silent on the ride back to Courtney's townhouse. In truth, they'd worn each other out at dinner. For every argument she raised, he retaliated with an equally cogent counter-argument. He kept harping about tobacco being the scapegoat for taxes and how it simply wasn't fair to levy exorbitant fees on a product that had been a staple of the American economy since the pilgrims planted the first crops in the seventeenth century. Generations of tobacco families had tilled the soil. They were part of the fabric of what made this country great.

Courtney's counter-argument focused on youth. If adults wanted to wreck their health, that was their business. But for kids as young as ten or twelve years old to be hooked on cigarettes before they had the good judgment or foresight to consider their health was an abomination. With higher taxes, fewer youth would be able to afford cigarettes, and the taxes could pay for a new anti-smoking campaign targeted at kids in elementary school.

She had to give him credit for at least listening to her. He nodded at the right parts, anyway. But Courtney couldn't see that he'd budged. She felt her hopes of ever convincing him fade as he pulled up in front of her townhouse.

"Would you like to come in?" she asked, though she wasn't sure why. She was pretty worn out from all the back and forth, but she hated to see the evening end. His sense of humor and intelligence were intoxicating.

"Thanks, but I've got an early morning." He smiled, but it didn't reach his eyes. He was probably just as weary as she was from their heated exchange. He moved his jaw around, like he was stifling a yawn.

Now I'm putting him to sleep. And glomming on to the fact that we're at an impasse on tobacco, he thinks I'm the world's biggest goody-two-shoes.

"Certainly, I understand." Courtney held up a hand. "Don't get out. I'll see myself to the door." *So, that's that.* What could she possibly do to leave an impression? *When all else fails, try shock value.* "Unless you'd like to see my drawer full of sex toys?"

His eyes grew wide, but only for a second. "Right, that sounds like you."

"You don't know everything about me." Courtney winked and then ran her finger across his lips. *Did I really do that?* Swinging her legs out the door, she said, "Goodnight, Eric," before slowly and seductively walking to her door, which wasn't easy considering the temperature was close to freezing and she felt more like running. She didn't look back; he'd have seen her teeth chattering. Well, let him chew on her parting statement for a while. It might warm him up, though in truth, the closest thing she had to sex toys was a vibrator with dead batteries.

Chapter Four

Eric couldn't concentrate. He stared at page one of the three hundred-page education bill, and his eyes glazed over. Courtney's parting comment swirled in his brain like the fudge in his favorite ripple ice cream. Was she serious about the sex toys? Was she really a virgin? He'd never encountered anyone even remotely like her. He slammed the bill closed. Courtney warranted some serious analysis. Time to make a list. He took the yellow legal pad from his desk and picked up a pencil.

The Id of Courtney:

1. She's smart, very smart.
2. She's completely committed to her cause, which shows her depth of character. She isn't simply hawking the party line, she's a true believer.
3. She's beautiful, though she isn't aware of it, which makes her all the more lovely.
4. She's genuine, the real McCoy, the kind of woman you'd take home to meet the parents.
5. She's sexy, though she hadn't turned it on until the end of the evening. It was more a wakeup call than a come hither.
6. What are her motives, aside from swaying a vote? Or is that all she's interested in? She isn't flirty, so why the parting come-on? Was it just a joke?
7. And if she's seriously into sex toys, would she be interested in role play? A blindfold? Handcuffs?

Eric's heart beat faster than it did after a quick run up the Capitol steps. He ripped the note off the legal pad, tore it into little pieces, and then emptied it into his trash. He considered eating the pieces, lest anyone reassemble them and read the sex toys part. All he'd need was for the media to get wind of his carnal desires. He'd been teasing about the riding crop, but she'd evidently taken him seriously. Playing the jockey to her Secretariat wasn't his idea of foreplay. If Courtney really had those sex toys, she had to be someone with a rich fantasy life. And if she was truly a virgin, her fantasies were probably all she had. He'd read that many women found the *Fifty Shades* books a turn on, but few actually wanted to experience BDSM. It certainly did nothing for him. Perhaps Courtney was a latent tigress, just itching to be set free. Once unleashed, she might be too wild, and that wouldn't bode well for his political future.

He needed to shelve this train of thought or he'd never get through this education bill. But before he dove back into work, he buzzed the intercom for his secretary.

"Lorena, can you get me Miss Larson's phone number, please?"

• • •

Courtney sat across from her roommate at Co Co Sala, the trendy D.C. lunch spot, absentmindedly picking at her chocolate torte.

"I can't believe you got a dessert for lunch," Helen said. "It's so not you, and chocolate, no less."

"Come on, Helen, you know you have to pry my hands off Three Musketeers."

"Yeah, but that's only after you've had a Lean Cuisine for dinner."

"Well, I'm a bit confused today. I'm eating dessert first." Courtney blinked around the busy restaurant like she was looking for a long-lost friend.

"You're distracted, that's for sure. Something the senator said last night?"

That slammed her back to the present. She propped her elbows on the table and her head in her hands. "It wasn't what he said; it was what *I* said. I couldn't keep my mouth shut."

"Yikes, Court. First dates aren't the place for true confessions. You're supposed to put your best foot forward."

"I did put my foot forward ... and then I stuck it in my mouth. He must think I'm schizophrenic."

"What did you say?" Helen leaned forward.

"I morphed from Snow White to Belle Watling in a matter of seconds."

"Who's Belle Watling?"

"You know, the hooker from *Gone With the Wind?* She was Rhett Butler's friend."

"Oh, yeah, I remember her. She had a good heart."

Courtney threw up her hands. "That's how I want to be remembered, as the hooker with the good heart."

"It could be worse. You could be Snow White, the anarchist."

"You're not helping."

"Okay, how about this? Why do you care? You've never been interested in *any* guy. I climb the walls when I need to get laid. You give yourself a pedicure. It's like men are superfluous for you."

"I've been telling you, Helen, you need a vibrator. Gets the job done without all those messy emotions."

"I wouldn't know how to use a vibrator. It would languish in my tool chest."

"And I thought we knew everything about each other. You have a tool chest?"

"Yes, I do. Let me know if you ever need a screwdriver." Helen narrowed her eyes. "We're off the subject. You haven't told me why this guy fascinates you."

Courtney tapped a finger to her lips. "Because under his façade of hot Washington player, I think there's a really nice guy. And besides, there's more to liking a man than wanting to jump into bed with him." Courtney shrugged. "But I'm still so emotional about my mom dying. I can't imagine investing that kind of feeling in a man. Bottom line, I'm afraid to."

"I'm not buying the fear argument. Remember what Eleanor Roosevelt said, and I'm paraphrasing, but it had to do with personal growth based on stretching boundaries and facing fears. Don't torture yourself over this man. Call him."

Courtney walked back to her office, hugging the storefronts to avoid the freezing rain. By the time she reached Montgomery, Haskins & Knoll, she wanted nothing more than to soak in a bath full of bubbles, but the afternoon held a stack of paperwork that threatened to implode her desk. Next time she was at Bed, Bath & Beyond, she'd pick up one of those over-the-tub writing desks so she could work while Calgon took her away. But for now, there was nothing to do but take off her galoshes and get a cup of coffee. She pondered Helen's suggestion to call Eric, but what would she say? "Hi, Courtney here, the crazy lobbyist who still holds her V-card. Remember me?"

Pencils sharpened, she settled into her work, but before she tuned everything out and focused, she allowed herself one fleeting thought of Eric. In her mind's eye, his lips turned up in a provocative smile, exposing his dimple. Damn, he was enticing, like the best fantasy ever. When she left Eric last night, she'd thrown out a hint. She wondered if it had left an itch in his craw.

Jumping when her phone buzzed, she stared at it a moment before hitting the speaker button. "Yes?"

"There's an Eric Morrison on line one for you." Elise's voice lilted playfully.

Courtney's windpipe constricted, and she had to gulp for air.

"This is Courtney." The "ney" sounded more like "neigh." When had she picked up a British accent?

"Hi, it's Eric." He cleared his throat. "How are you?"

"Fine." Her tone was brisk, clipped, to make sure her voice didn't quake.

"Working hard?"

"Yes."

"Too hard to spare me an evening?"

"No."

"Great. How about tonight?"

"Sure."

"I'll pick you up at eight."

"Right." She hung up. She couldn't remember the last time she'd had a monosyllabic conversation with anyone. Oh, yeah, it had been with her dad, not long after her mom passed. She hadn't wanted him to hear her voice crack. He'd had enough grief of his own to deal with.

Tears welled in Courtney's eyes. The tobacco campaign had provided a way to honor her mother's memory. She'd been hell-bent on securing Eric Morrison's vote, and now all she wanted was to see him again. Where was her dogged determination?

She took a tissue from her desk drawer, dabbed at her eyes, and sniffled. She was tougher than this. She'd concentrate on the other votes she needed and then she'd circle back with Eric Morrison once she had some momentum under her belt. In the meantime, she'd try to enjoy being with Eric, the charismatic man. She promised herself she'd bite her tongue if she talked politics tonight.

What would she wear? Helen had a hot pink sweater dress that she said she'd lend if Courtney would reciprocate with her ankle boots. Yeah, that's the ticket. She'd already tried on the dress. It hugged her curves, and paired with textured stockings and pumps, it would be sexy, yet demure—just right for a virgin into sex toys. Speaking of which, what would Eric be expecting? And could she possibly live up to his expectations? He was so calm and collected, a sophisticated man of the world. She'd been provocative, but did he see past the veneer to the sexual novice she truly was? Sure, they'd tantalized each other with talk about riding crops and sex toys, but if she were pressed to come up with a collection of sexual accoutrements, she'd have to march out her lucite statue of the Washington Monument. While phallic, it would be a stretch as a sex toy.

And rather painful.

But maybe he'd like that.

Good grief, she'd never get out of the office if she didn't buckle down. She'd worry later about her evening with Eric. For now, the stack of paperwork screamed for attention.

Chapter Five

Eric leaned back in his chair and almost toppled over. He grabbed the edge of his desk to steady himself. Well, that was an interesting conversation, if you could call it that. He couldn't tell whether Courtney was happy to hear from him or terrified. She'd said all of five words, but the most important one had been "yes," so in the aggregate, he'd have to put the call in the plus column. And in just a few hours, he'd see her. So much for his "never date a lobbyist" rule. He'd let down his guard ... big time.

Oh, God, was he reading too much into her sex toy confession? Or was she just like him, a collector who'd never actually used the paraphernalia? He was reminded of a friend in high school who collected Star Trek sabers. Just because he could swing one around didn't mean he was Luke Skywalker.

He had to admit he loved the juxtaposition of a straight-laced woman with a tigress in the bedroom. He pictured her dressed like a schoolmarm, with her hair pulled back in a bun and her feet laced in matronly oxfords. She'd sit primly in a chair, smoothing down her long skirt, but underneath, she'd wear crotch-less panties.

Was Courtney the woman of his dreams?

Maybe he'd be too tame for her.

Tonight he'd find out.

• • •

He arrived at her townhouse promptly at eight. Blowing on his fingers, he tightened the scarf around his neck just as the door opened.

My, my, she was gorgeous, all pink, feminine, and hot. She was the kind of woman who made a man's chest puff with pride.

"You look incredible," he said.

"Thanks." She ducked her head a bit. "Where're we going tonight?"

"I thought I'd subject you to my cooking, if that's all right." He hadn't cooked for a woman since he'd last been home. And that woman was his mother.

"That's fine, but where did you find the time?" She motioned him into the foyer.

"I had some serious help from the gourmet market on the corner. Actually, about all I have to do is warm things up." *I'd like to warm you up.*

"Nonetheless, I'm impressed." She retrieved her coat from the hall closet.

"Don't be … yet."

They caught up with each other's day on the way to Eric's apartment in Arlington. Courtney mentioned three senatorial meetings, though she kept it vague as to the content. Maybe she'd decided to keep tobacco out of the conversation for the evening. That was a good sign.

"Aren't you a bit out of the action here?" Courtney asked as they pulled into Eric's underground garage.

"I'm just around the corner from the Clarendon Metro, so it's an easy train ride downtown. Besides, I love the history in Arlington. And being close to the national cemetery keeps me humble. If I start to get a big head about being a senator, I remind myself that what I'm doing can't begin to compare to the sacrifices some people have made."

Courtney pursed her lips, no doubt appraising him. He hated to waste that sweet pucker, but he'd bide his time.

"Hope that didn't sound sanctimonious," Eric said.

"No, I know exactly how you feel. Sometimes I walk around Georgetown like I own the place just because I went to school there. And then I remember something my mother always said— that we're on this earth to serve others, not to be served." Courtney laughed. "Of course, being the oldest child with two younger, very messy, brothers prepared me for a life of service. I started picking up after them when I was five."

"And may I say how very much we younger brothers appreciate our older sisters? Although there was a method to my sister's selflessness—when Jennifer was picking up after me, she made sure Mom knew what a mess I'd made."

Courtney's eyes crinkled as she smiled. "Reporting is part of the job."

"I suppose. My sister kept a list of my infractions."

They took the elevator from the garage to the sixth floor where the doors opened to a central hallway that accessed four apartment doors. Eric opened his door and motioned for Courtney to go in ahead of him. His housekeeper had been there just that morning, so he felt confident that his usual detritus of *Wall St. Journals* and *Washington Posts* were in the recycling bin. She would also have run and emptied his dishwasher, which, with his busy schedule, only filled up once a week.

They were interrupted by a squeaky whine.

"What's that?" Courtney asked.

"It's kind of a dog." Eric backed away from her and into the kitchen. He motioned for her to follow. "She's in a kennel in the laundry room. I'm house training her, and it's been a nightmare. The only saving grace is that her puddles are so small, the mess is minimal."

He opened the door to reveal his stacked washer and dryer, a washtub, and a large kennel that housed a tiny dog.

"Chihuahua?" Courtney asked, squatting in front of the cage and pressing her fingers to the wire bars. She looked back at Eric. "It takes a real man to have a Chihuahua. You must eat quiche, too."

"My sexuality has never been in question." He nodded to the little dog. "Her name's Pinky."

Pinky stuck her tongue through the wires to lick Courtney.

"Can I let her out?" Courtney didn't wait for Eric's reply. She opened the cage door and scooped up the dog. "Oh, she's adorable." Courtney lifted the dog to her face, at which point Pinky plastered her ears against her head and tried desperately to lick up Courtney's nose.

"Be careful. She'd adept at maneuvering that little tongue up a nostril. So far, my little friend Travis is the only willing subject." Eric tickled the dog's rump. "I grew up with Chihuahuas, beagles, and mutts. Sometimes we'd get a very interesting combination if we didn't get them neutered soon enough. You don't see many Chihuahuas who bay at the moon like a hound, but we had one." Eric checked his watch. "I need to oversee things in the kitchen. Want a glass of wine?"

"Sure," Courtney said. She took Pinky into the living room and sat down on the floor with her.

Eric watched them from the kitchen while he poured two glasses of Pinot noir and stuck the pork tenderloin and asparagus in the preheated oven to warm. God, Courtney was beautiful, and she seemed comfortable around him. His heart thumped.

During dinner, they shared LSAT scores (Courtney's were slightly higher), favorite movies (*Shakespeare in Love* and *Love Actually* for Courtney, *Saving Private Ryan* and *Clear and Present Danger* for Eric), best childhood memories (Sea World for Courtney, Civil War battlefields for Eric), and they polished off a bottle of wine.

"Would you like some Courvoisier or Drambuie?" Eric asked after they'd cleared the table.

"Drambuie would be great," Courtney replied. "I'll just use the ladies' room first."

"First door on the right off the hall," Eric said. He poured the liqueur in brandy snifters and took the drinks to the coffee table.

• • •

Courtney started to re-apply her lipstick in the bathroom mirror and then stopped her hand midstream. What if he wanted to kiss her? She switched to a pale pink gloss and applied it sparingly. Her head throbbed. The wine had contributed, but mostly her nerves had seized up. She knew you weren't supposed to take ibuprofen when you'd been drinking, but if she could find some, her liver would just have to cope. She looked first in the recessed medicine chest on the wall. Finding nothing there, she opened the cabinet below the sink. She rifled among the prescription bottles, most of which were expired antibiotics and flu remedies. No ibuprofen, but as she was about to close the cabinet, something pink and silky caught her eye. She retrieved a pair of bikini panties; no, make that a thong. She forgot about her headache. She replaced the thong and closed the cabinet door. Passing by an open door on the way back to the living room, she stopped to peek inside what appeared to be Eric's home office. He hadn't been kidding about his collection. An entire wall was chock full of framed riding crops and dressage whips, a few of which looked antique, like from a previous century, or perhaps from a museum of sex? Courtney pressed her fingers to her temples. Her head pounded. Was she scared or excited? How about both?

She returned to the living room where Eric waited, proffering a brandy snifter. She took it, swirled the thick amber liquid, and inhaled the warm aroma of the Drambuie. Her heart was beating out of her chest as she took a tentative sip of her drink. Would this be the night she lost her virginity? She couldn't deny her attraction to Eric, but beyond the dastardly deed, was she ready to be that close to him? Her body tingled all over, so that was all systems go, but a little voice in her head urged caution. She thought about what advice Helen would offer at a time like this. No doubt, Helen would say it was time to put up or shut up.

Courtney started to take another sip of her drink, but Eric took the glass out of her hand and set it on the coffee table. Then he pulled her into his arms. When his lips met hers, they were oh, so soft as he traced a slow journey inside her bottom lip with his tongue. He was an expert, and she followed his lead. Nothing invasive about this kiss, just sensual and slow. She spread her fingers over his solid back, feeling his muscles flex. This was the best kiss of her life, and she wanted it to last. She eased her hands up to his neck where her fingers on the prickly little hairs above his sweater made them both shiver. They continued their slow kiss, nipping and tasting. While the feelings coursing through her body were insanely pleasurable, a wave of panic suddenly gripped her. She'd never been this close to surrender.

Abruptly, Courtney ended the kiss and looked deeply into Eric's eyes. "I've never wanted to have sex this badly in my life." *Helen would be proud of me.*

Eric drew a deep breath, and then blew it out slowly. "Do you want to have sex with me, Courtney?"

"Honestly, I'm not really sure." Courtney chewed on her bottom lip. "I just know my body is a jumble of nerve endings, and they're all firing."

"I want to make love to you, Courtney, but I'm not going to until you're sure it's what you want. What you're sacrificing means more than that."

Courtney took a few shallow breaths. She pressed a hand to her heart. He hadn't said 'sex,' he'd said 'love.' *Whoa.* She needed his touch, even if it was just a brush of his fingers across her cheek.

Eric took her hand, and they stared into each other's eyes, both steadying their breathing.

"I'm afraid we'll get carried away if I kiss you again." One side of his mouth turned up in a grin.

"We would." Courtney shivered, whether from disappointment or Eric's save, she wasn't sure. "I'm going to need to lose it sometime."

"Yeah, but it needs to be with someone you really care about. The first time can be awkward, but if it's with someone special, it can also be magical." He touched her cheek gently. "The truth is, we barely know each other. There's no rush."

Courtney knew Eric was right. She'd been so ready to throw caution to the wind, but her hormones had at least fizzled to the point where her head could take over. Warmth spread through her limbs, and it wasn't from the Drambuie. It was the abiding warmth of gratitude, tinged with a dose of embarrassment. "I, I think I should go home now."

Chapter Six

"I'm glad to see you're back to soup for lunch, instead of chocolate." Helen added another teaspoon of sugar to her chai tea at their usual haunt, Co Co Sala.

"I could live on soup. It's the world's most perfect food." Courtney blew on her spoonful of beef barley, though she still yearned for chocolate.

"And sounds to me like you've found the world's most perfect man," Helen said.

"Yeah, it's been two weeks since the big reveal, and he's still around." Courtney shook her head. "But we're sticking to coffee shops, art museums, and the zoo. Places where we can't get into an intimate conversation."

"The zoo is especially good. Coffee shops can be intimate and there's always something erotic at an art museum, but animal sex isn't much of a turn on. 'Oh, Eric, look at the rhinoceroses humping. Let's go home and get it on.'" Helen sipped her tea. "But you're avoiding the inevitable."

Courtney looked at Helen sideways. "I think the plural is rhinoceri, but what do you mean by inevitable?"

"I mean, you like this guy."

"Oh, criminy, I know. And I want to melt into him. I want to snuggle into his chest and breathe him into me so that we become one person."

"Okay, aside from the fact that *sex* would do that, what's your problem?"

"What if I'm way too tame for him? I've never done this before. What if I freeze up in bed with him? What if I'm a vanilla-sex girl?"

"Maybe he's worried about the same thing. He's got toys, but has he used them?" Helen patted Courtney's hand. "Look, the first time for sex is like jumping in a frigid lake, but once you get past the initial plunge, the pleasure takes over. Don't worry about it so much, Court. You're not a vanilla girl. I'd peg you for Cherry Garcia. Lots of bursts of flavor, that's you."

"Easy for you to say! What if *I'm* the frigid lake?"

"Well, you like this guy right? I mean, sex aside?"

"Yes, I *like* Eric. I more than like him. I find myself thinking about him *all the time*, and I've *never* felt that way about a man. He's everything I never wanted."

"Huh?"

"I didn't realize falling for someone could be such a major distraction," she shook her head. "The vote's fast approaching and I still need two more senate votes.

"Yeah, and you don't even have Eric's yet," Helen pointed out.

"I'm working hard on everyone else. Maybe I can turn someone. It's great that this tax is bipartisan. It provides an opportunity for both parties to finally agree on something. "

"Have you given up on convincing Eric? It could be a post-coital bargaining chip?" Helen waggled her eyebrows.

"I hope you're kidding. I would never do that."

"Of course, I'm kidding, although he may think you're sticking around just to take another stab at swaying his vote."

"I'm sticking around until I blow it, which I inevitably will."

"Why do you say that?"

"Because I really don't know what I'm doing."

• • •

Eric was used to linear relationships. Not that he had a checklist for the steps to take, but he typically didn't start with a major confession and then work backwards—at least not until he met

Courtney. But damn, no woman had ever intrigued him like this. He'd butt heads with her any day on congressional issues, where she was more than capable of holding her own. But in terms of sex, she was a babe in the woods. And except for his first sexual encounter—at age fifteen with his equally inexperienced girlfriend—it had been at least ten years since he'd dated a virgin. Whoa. That revelation travelled to his heart. The prospect of being Courtney's first lover made him feel … special.

They'd spent the last two weeks being safe, only going to places where they weren't alone. Hell, he hadn't even kissed her. And the longer he waited, the more nervous he became. Tonight, they were meeting for a drink on the mezzanine at the Mayflower Hotel. It would be the most intimate setting he'd dared—since his apartment. Elegant, yet cozy. He planned to scout out a secluded table before she arrived. They'd only have time for a brief drink as they both had work engagements elsewhere, but he hoped there'd be a moment for a kiss … or two.

• • •

Eric tapped his foot under the cocktail table. He'd arrived early, which was totally out of character, and had already ordered two glasses of pinot grigio. He downed half of his by the time Courtney arrived.

"Hi." She slid into a red leather bucket chair.

Eric handed her the wine glass and then scooted his chair closer. "Hi. You look flustered." Her cheekbones held splotches of red.

"I had three congressional appointments today. Every one of the legislators was late, and I had the fight of my life with one of them. You know how that goes." She swirled the wine in the glass and then took a sip. "Nice bouquet. You know your grapes, Senator."

He much preferred when she called him Eric. "Thanks. We have a winery on the farm. The grapes are in a valley between the tobacco barns." As soon as he mentioned tobacco, he wished he hadn't.

"I like to forget you're from a tobacco family." She didn't smile.

"Sometimes, like right now, so do I." He ventured a brief grin.

She sighed. "Sorry, it's been a long day, and I'm being too sensitive. But before we get off the subject, did you ever smoke?"

"No. No one in my family smokes now, though my grandparents did—like chimneys."

"What happened to them?" Courtney looked him directly in the eyes.

Eric ducked his head. "They both died of emphysema." He remembered his grandmother's labored breathing, and his heart clenched. He shook the memory, not wanting to dwell on the pain.

"And you wonder why I'm on this campaign?" Courtney crossed one leg over the other and jiggled her foot.

"I know precisely why you're taking a stance for higher taxes. I simply don't agree."

"How can you think like that when your grandparents died as a direct result of smoking?"

"Courtney, we've been over this. I'm supporting my constituents."

"And you're killing the rest of us."

"Could we please not talk about tobacco?"

Courtney glared at him. The tips of her ears turned red.

"You're losing perspective, Courtney."

She continued to glare. Her foot jiggle reverberated up her leg.

"I was hoping for a pleasant, relaxing conversation, a few stolen moments before I have to be on stage again" He tried to smile, but his jaw was tense. It probably came off as a sneer.

"This wasn't a good idea." She contemplated the Greek friezes on the mezzanine wall. "Maybe *we're* not a good idea."

"Don't jump to conclusions. Why don't you go home and soak in a tub?" He cringed. He'd meant to suggest she do something nice for herself, but it came out sounding more like, "Why don't you take a long walk off a short pier?"

"And why don't you cut off your nose to spite your face?" Tears welled in her eyes. "That's what you're doing with this tobacco bill. You say you're helping your constituents, but will they thank you in the long run ... when they're dying?" Her voice rose an octave. She swiped at her tears.

"Courtney, please don't take this personally. I know this is about your mom, but you can't get so worked up over it."

"Why not? What *else* should I get worked up over?"

"Well, since you asked ..." Eric grinned, which she probably read as lascivious. All he'd wanted was a few moments of closeness, and he botched it with sexual innuendo. Damn if he didn't just come across like a snarling wolf. "Courtney, I'm sorry. That was crude, and I didn't mean to downplay your feelings."

"Didn't you?" She pushed herself out of the chair. "Thanks for the drink." She stormed out and didn't look back.

• • •

Courtney rushed to the street and hailed a cab. When she gave the cabbie her destination, the Dirty Martini, he informed her that it was just a short walk from the Mayflower. She thanked him and pulled her camel hair coat tighter around her. Tears flowed down her cheeks. She hiked up Connecticut Avenue, chiding herself with each slap of boot on pavement. She'd let the day get to her and then Eric had been a complete jerk. They'd had an opportunity to really talk, and he completely blew it. Thank goodness Helen would be at this event tonight. Her *pro bono* work as a guardian *ad litem* often put them in the same places at the same time. She needed to vent.

She elbowed her way into the restaurant/bar, which was already jammed. An old Bob Seger song, "Still the Same," played in the background. The Dirty Martini was a popular spot for political and non-profit events, and tonight's fundraiser had really packed the huge space. She squeezed her way to the bar, but was directed by the bartender to a waiter holding a silver tray laden with champagne flutes above his head. "There's going to be a toast first," he'd told her. She held up her hand to the waiter, and he made his way to her. Lowering the tray, Courtney chose the fullest flute.

A poke in her ribs jerked her head to the left. Helen pointed to a space at the end of the bar, and the two women shimmied through the crowd.

"Whew," Helen said. "I think they're going to corral us into a private space soon, but it wasn't ready when I came in."

"How long have you been here?"

"Let's see, this is my third champagne, so about half an hour." Helen blinked. "Did the cat drag you in? I thought you'd be all bouncy and glowing from your meeting with Eric."

"It was awful. I'd get drunk, but I've got too much work to do." Courtney rolled her eyes, and then caught her reflection in the huge mirror behind the bar. She *did* look horrendous.

"Oh, get drunk anyway. Sometimes it's the only remedy." Helen took another swig.

Courtney downed her flute in two gulps and then let Helen pull her toward another room where a *maître d'* was corralling patrons. She picked up another glass on the way in.

About fifty people milled around a long buffet table. A woman in a red suit stepped up on a riser at one end of the room.

She tapped the podium microphone, which made a popping sound and got everyone's attention. "Welcome, everyone. I'm

Rebecca Arch, executive director of the Special Olympics, and I'm so pleased to see you here this evening. I'm particularly pleased to welcome a senator who's no stranger to our cause. He spearheaded Project UNIFY in his home state of North Carolina. Would you raise your glasses in a toast to Senator Eric Morrison?"

Courtney stiffened. She'd forgotten Eric was involved in Special Olympics. Heck, she'd forgotten what the event benefitted. Where was her head? *And why didn't he tell me he was coming here tonight? 'Course, I didn't tell him where I was going either.*

"As many of you know," Ms. Arch continued, "Special Olympics Project UNIFY is a series of innovative activities through which public and private schools can become more involved in Special Olympics through a variety of youth leadership activities, sports, and awareness activities. But I'll let Senator Morrison tell you about the difference Project UNIFY has made in his state. Senator?"

Courtney wanted to crawl under the nearest table. A punch to her elbow signified that Helen was on board. She whispered in Courtney's ear. "I'll prop you up if you get woozy."

"You're woozier than me," Courtney said.

"Yeah, but I'm not in *lurve*."

"Neither am I," Courtney said, though her heart wasn't cooperating. She could hear it beating in her ears. And her knees wobbled. She took a swig of champagne and watched Eric bound up to the podium. She hadn't had time to properly admire his wardrobe at the Mayflower, but he looked gorgeous in his navy wool suit, light blue shirt, and maroon and blue striped tie. She took a deep breath and blew it out through puffed cheeks.

"Good evening, and thank you, Rebecca, for the wonderful work you do every day for Special Olympics." Courtney froze when he made eye contact with her. He cleared his throat and continued to look directly at her. "In spite of people in this room who are on opposite sides of issues, I think we can all agree that the Special Olympics knows no dissension."

Duly noted, Courtney rubbed the back of her hand, like she'd been swatted with a ruler by a nun in parochial school. She knew Eric was right. She'd never have had such an outburst with anyone else. He was entitled to his opinion, but what galled her was that if he was so philanthropic and cognizant of the underdog, why couldn't he see that the only good tobacco was a shriveled crop? She couldn't stay here and listen to this. She turned to Helen. "I'm leaving."

"No, you can't. That would be over-the-top rude to leave in the middle of his speech."

"I know. It's rude and cowardly, and I'm doing it." She hurried out of the room and back through the main bar, where the sound system piped out a Linda Ronstadt tune, "Somewhere Out There." Her mom had loved that song. Courtney's eyes welled with tears as she tore out of the bar.

• • •

Following his remarks from the podium, Eric searched the room for Courtney. He approached the woman he'd seen her standing with. "Hi," he said, "did Courtney leave?"

"Hi, yourself. I'm Court's roommate, Helen." She held out her hand, and Eric shook it. "She, uh, wasn't feeling well. She just left."

"Sure it didn't have something to do with me?"

"Now why would you think that?" Helen looked at Eric, but she didn't maintain eye contact. She scanned the room and then returned to his face. "Don't give up on her."

Eric ran a hand through his hair and kept it at the back of his neck. "I wasn't planning to, but she's not making it easy." He dropped his hand.

"I don't want to talk out of school here, but from what she's told me, you seem to be a good guy. She deserves a good guy."

Helen put her hand on Eric's sleeve. "It probably seems like she's sabotaging things, but she doesn't really want to."

"I've never met anyone like her."

"Yeah, that's our Court. She's an original." Helen sipped her champagne.

"Anytime we broach the subject of tobacco, she gets so emotional that we can't talk rationally about it." Eric shook his head.

Helen gave him a considering look, as if deciding something, then leaned close. "Look, don't tell her I told you any of this, but when her mom died, she was heavy into school, and she didn't let herself grieve. Now, her job focus is a constant reminder that her mother died from cigarettes. So, she's finally working through all that repressed sorrow." Helen's eyes narrowed like she was sizing him up. "Want some advice?"

"I'd love some."

"You really want to get through to Court? Show her who you really are. You're into the environment, right? Take her to a landfill."

Eric's eyebrows climbed in confusion.

"Okay, no, I'm just kidding," Helen chuckled. "But take her somewhere away from this D.C. frenzy, where she won't be tempted to talk politics. If you can open up to her, maybe she can finally open up to you." She winked. "In more ways than one, if you get my drift."

From his mood of discouragement, Eric emerged with new resolve. Helen was right, and he'd been an idiot not to be more considerate of Courtney's grief. He couldn't wait to make it up to her.

Chapter Seven

Saturday morning, Courtney watched for Eric through the skinny window that bordered her front door. When his car pulled up to her curb—double parking of course, since you could never find a spot on the street in Foggy Bottom—the flutters in her stomach floated all the way to her heart.

While the weather had been abysmal most of the winter, today's expected high was mid-60s, boding well for a picnic and tour of the Manassas Battlefield with Travis, Eric's Little Brother. Eric had told her he spent one weekend a month with Travis, and she was thrilled to be involved in today's outing. This could be a good opportunity to put her crusade aside and just have a good time, if she could keep her mouth shut about tobacco ... for once.

When she'd told Helen about the upcoming excursion, her friend had grinned like the happy Buddha statue that sat in a potted plant on her windowsill. Helen had spent an evening with Courtney extolling Eric's virtues, and her persuasive powers (she wasn't a litigator for nothing) had convinced Courtney that he probably was a great guy.

Courtney had packed a picnic lunch. "I brought enough to feed an elephant, but I know how boys can eat," she said, sliding into the passenger seat. Eric set the picnic basket in the backseat.

"Travis is small for his age, but he can pack it away. And then there's me." Eric smiled.

God, Helen was right; he was yummy. When he smiled, the air around him vibrated with sheer pleasure. "And with the chill in the air, I think that makes everyone hungrier. I've got a thermos of hot chocolate, too."

Before they reached McLean to pick up Travis, Eric told Courtney about the little boy he'd been mentoring for two years.

"He's shy, but there are a few subjects he'll open up about, like puppies and basketball."

"Too bad you couldn't bring Pinky," Courtney said.

"Oh, he loves her. He's spending the weekend at my place, so he'll get plenty of her."

Could I ever get plenty of you? Courtney gazed at Eric's strong profile while he drove with his left hand on the wheel and the right resting on the leather seat. She wanted to reach over and intertwine her fingers with his. "When I knew we were going to Manassas, I looked up the battlefield online to see if they had any activities for kids. They participate in the National Park Service's Junior Ranger program. My brothers used to love the Junior Ranger books. You have to complete a number of activities, and then they give you a badge."

"Travis will enjoy that. He's all about showing me what he can do. At first, he didn't care. He'd been shuffled around to so many places he didn't trust anyone."

"What happened to his parents?"

"His dad died of a drug overdose, and his mom just dropped him off at the Department of Social Services one day and split town. He's in a decent foster home now, but he doesn't let his heart get attached. I'm the one constant in his life."

"That's a big responsibility." *Poor little guy.* Courtney blinked hard as tears built behind her eyes. She bit her lip to keep them at bay.

"He's special. You'll see."

• • •

Travis obviously loved Eric. Bounding to the car like he'd been let out of San Quentin, the boy hopped into the backseat and immediately buckled himself in. "See, you didn't have to tell me to use my seatbelt."

"You've got a good memory, Travis," Eric said as he pulled away from the modest house on the outskirts of McLean, waving to Travis's foster mom, who stood at the door. "Hope you don't mind that I brought my friend, Courtney. She's been keeping an eye on me, making sure I stay in line."

Yeah, like she could keep Eric in line. Courtney turned around in her seat. The smile on the little boy's face could light the National Mall. "Thanks for letting me tag along today, Travis. I've missed being around boys. I have two younger brothers, but I don't see them much anymore."

"What happened to them?" Travis's smile dissolved, and the corners of his mouth turned down.

Oh, no, I hope I didn't strike a sad chord. Maybe he thinks they're in juvenile detention. "They grew up."

"I'm gonna do that someday." The smile returned, and Travis pounded the back of Eric's car seat. "Hey, did I tell ya that I got an 'A' on my history test? I'm thinkin' I might grow up to be a senator."

"That would be super, buddy," Eric said, putting on his sunglasses. "Just remember that if you decide to go into politics, the most important thing is to represent the people from your district."

"What's that mean?" Travis asked.

"It means that you have to listen to them, and when you go to Washington, you fight for what they need back home." He glanced at Courtney over the top of his sunglasses.

She stiffened. "That's right, Travis, although as a senator, you have to be the leader. When the people you're representing are heading in the wrong direction, you have to steer them toward what's best for them." She felt heat creep up her neck. *Oh, no, I told myself I wasn't going to get all preachy about tobacco. Back off, Court.*

Eric cleared his throat. "You can't treat your constituents like children, Travis. You have to trust that they put you in Congress, and you're there to support the causes they believe in."

"Yes, but you have to look to the future, to what will keep people and the planet healthy. What folks want today may not be the best choices for the future." Courtney's volume escalated. She'd soon drown out the voice of Carrie Underwood on Eric's radio. *What's wrong with me? Can't I relax?* She took a deep breath. She needed to tape her mouth shut.

"I don't know what you two are talkin' about, but it sounds like somebody's gettin' mad," Travis said. He looked back and forth between Eric and Courtney.

Courtney stole a glance at Eric. "I'm sorry we got off on this, Travis. We're not mad, but we do have a difference of opinion about something that we both care deeply about."

"Well, heck, that's life." Travis, the philosopher, shrugged.

Eric laughed. "You're right, buddy. We can't agree about everything."

Courtney rolled her shoulders, which she realized were scrunched up under her ears.

Eric reached for her hand and held it on the console between them. "I was hoping this day would be fun for all of us."

She'd been craving the warmth of his hand, and it didn't disappoint. From the tips of her fingers, the warmth spread up her arm and to her heart. "Me, too, and I promise—no more talk about work. Not today." Her lips quivered a bit as she smiled. She hoped Eric hadn't noticed, and really, she wasn't sure whether the quiver was from the heat of their discussion or the electricity of his touch.

The rest of the day was picture perfect. Eric and Courtney walked the battlefield, sharing childhood stories, while Travis ran from tree to tree, pretending he was sneaking up on enemy troops. They all participated in a scavenger hunt to find objects around the Visitors' Center that counted toward Travis earning his Junior Ranger badge. After lunch, Eric and Courtney sat at the picnic bench, sipping hot chocolate, while Travis lingered in the shop, deciding what souvenir to buy with the five dollars Courtney had given him.

Sitting next to Eric on the picnic bench, Courtney wanted to slide her hand inside Eric's leather jacket and press her hand to his heart. She remembered asking her mother how she knew her father was "the one," and her mom said it was the day she wanted to feel his heartbeat. They'd been sitting in the bleachers after football practice. Her dad had his football helmet tucked under his arm, and he was winded when he sat down next to Courtney's mom. She said she knew she loved him because all she could think about was that she wanted his heart to beat for her. Is that what Courtney felt? Surely, it was too soon to feel this way.

On the way home, Travis snoozed in the backseat, and Courtney and Eric rode silently so they didn't wake him. Through a stroke of luck, a parking space was open in front of her townhouse, and Eric pulled into it. He walked Courtney to the door, and she found herself not wanting to say goodbye. She fumbled through her purse for her keys.

"Aren't you gonna kiss her?" Travis yelled from the car.

Courtney looked up at Eric.

"We can't disappoint the boy," he said.

"Surely not," Courtney agreed.

Eric put the picnic basket on the stoop, took Courtney's purse from her, and laid it on top of the basket. Wrapping one arm around her waist, he threaded his fingers through the hair at the back of her neck and pulled her into him, pressing their bodies tightly together. He kissed her temple, breathing into her hair. "Let me make myself clear, Courtney. I'm not doing this to please Travis."

She looked up into his clear eyes, the flecks of gold more prominent this close. "Neither am I."

"Maybe we should move out of his line of vision."

"Good idea." Courtney gave Eric a quick peck on the cheek, and then she opened her front door, took his hand and pulled him into her townhouse. She waved goodbye to Travis, and then shut the door.

Courtney was already breathing heavily when she stepped into Eric's embrace. She gazed up at him. "Okay, pal, work your magic." She closed her eyes, and he began to nibble on her bottom lip, sucked it into his mouth and bit, ever so gently. She moaned. She already knew he was a good kisser, but she wasn't prepared for this sensory explosion. She opened her mouth, and he shifted his lips to enclose hers. He traced his tongue sensuously inside her lips, and when he found the tip of her tongue, he pressed his to it like they were the last two pieces in a jigsaw puzzle, ensuring the perfect fit. Then he began a slow exploration, swirling and winding, but not deeply. Eric's tongue didn't assault, it invited. And together, their tongues melted in a harmonious dance. Rather than feeling invaded, Courtney wanted to deepen the experience. She kneaded the back of his neck, intertwining her fingers in his hair.

He pressed hard against her, lifting her off her feet so she could feel his erection pulse against her stomach.

Eric must have remembered he had a ten-year-old waiting in the car because he loosened his embrace and ended the kiss with a sweet, final peck. He rested his face against her ear, his breathing ragged and deep. "You're killing me," he whispered in her ear.

"To be continued?" She touched his lips, which were slightly swollen and also a bit pink from her lipstick.

"I've got Travis for the weekend and a work obligation on Monday. Are you free on Tuesday?"

"I am," she said, "and this time, I'll bring the riding crop."
She opened the door and touched Eric's cheek. His wide eyes and
slightly ajar mouth telegraphed anticipation.

She closed the door and collapsed against it, breathing heavily.
What had she done?

Chapter Eight

Helen pulled down the sash on the window blinds so hard that a cloud of dust flew off the sill, which sent her into a sneezing fit. She wiped her nose on the sleeve of her Hello Kitty robe, and said, "You told him *what?*"

Courtney crossed her arms over her nondescript pink pajamas. "I said I'd bring a riding crop."

"Girl, I've got to hand it to you. You're finally taking the plunge."

Courtney picked up the teapot she'd just brought to their bedroom and poured them each a cup. As was their custom, Sunday morning was devoted to tea and a leisurely read of the *Washington Post*.

"I need to get to the bottom of what he's really expecting." Courtney picked up her cup of tea and blew on the surface as she walked to the window of their second-story bedroom and looked across the miniscule front yard to the banks of melting snow in the street. "If he wants a whips-and-chains sex goddess, he's gonna be disappointed."

Helen dumped two teaspoons of sugar in her tea. "Are you sure you're ready? I know I said you should just go for it, but you gotta be sure."

Courtney chewed on her lip. "Honestly? Maybe I'm just a little bit ... scared shitless about having sex for the first time." She shrugged. "I mean, it's only been a few months since I was the nerd of the universe."

"Well, sex is a no-brainer, and it may surprise you to know that even nerds get down and dirty.... Once the heat is on, nature takes over." Helen sighed. "At any rate, you won't be in suspense too much longer. Tuesday night, right?"

"Yeah, his place, but he's not cooking this time. He said we're just going to order out for pizza—if we get that far."

• • •

Courtney dressed comfortably in J. Crew leggings and a cowl-necked burgundy cashmere sweater. She'd already pictured herself curled up on the sofa with her legs tucked under her, and this outfit was perfect. What she hadn't anticipated was the candle-light. It wasn't over-the-top like a romantic scene in the movies, where it looked like Yankee Candle had set up shop in someone's bedroom, but Eric had chosen one light, woodsy scent and placed a few strategic votives around the room, so the effect was subtle—and sexy. He wore distressed cords and a caramel-colored crew-neck sweater with the sleeves pushed up to his elbows, and he was barefoot, which Courtney also found somehow hot.

"You look gorgeous," he said. "Of course, you always look, and smell, incredible." He bent to her neck and inhaled.

She had to remind herself to breathe. "It's *J'adore*. Helen said I smelled like old books when I first moved in, so she made me upgrade." She looked up into his gold-flecked eyes. "And that color is great on you. It brings out the amber in your eyes."

"Thanks," he said. "The sweater was a gift from my mom." He froze. "Oh, I—"

Courtney touched his cheek. "I'm all right. If I cried every time someone mentioned their mother, I'd be in worse shape than I am." She smiled. "Where's Pinky?"

"I farmed her out to Travis for a week. Thought a bit of responsibility would be good for him, and some unconditional love from a Chihuahua never hurts, either. Travis is in a decent foster situation, but I know he still feels displaced."

"That was sweet of you."

Eric ducked his head a bit. "Wine?" He asked as he took her coat and hung it in his hall closet.

"I'd rather have bourbon." Courtney needed a jolt to steady her nerves, something that would go to her head quickly.

"I wouldn't have figured you for a bourbon woman." Eric squinted at Courtney like he was trying to see into her head. "Maker's Mark all right?"

"Perfect, and make it a double, please." Courtney headed to the couch. She set her purse on the coffee table, making sure the riding crop wasn't poking out the top, trying to escape. She tried to assume a relaxed posture by draping her arm over the back. Okay, that was a tad masculine. She plopped her hands in her lap and fiddled with her opal ring. She practiced deep breathing while Eric went to the kitchen for their libations. He returned a few minutes later with two crystal glasses. The amber bourbon shone like a beacon in the candlelight. They clinked glasses, and Courtney stifled a cough on the first sip.

"That's ... good. Kind of hits the back of your throat, though." Her voice was scratchy.

"Take it easy. It can creep up on you." Eric sat on the opposite side of the sofa, angling himself toward Courtney.

Courtney took another sip, and then closed her eyes while she pondered her approach. "The weather's been, oh, I don't know, would you say cold?"

Eric's eyebrows shot up. Maybe he had been expecting more than chitchat. "Uh, yes, I believe most meteorologists would use that scientific term—cold." He smiled.

"Yep, cold." Courtney pointed a finger in the air. "And windy, quite windy."

"Uh-huh."

"Help me out here, Senator."

"Okay, let's see, it's also been icy."

Well, this was silly. He was obviously following her lead, and it wasn't getting her anywhere. She reached for her purse, and without fanfare, extracted the riding crop.

If she thought his eyebrows shop up before, now they escaped into his hairline. He rubbed his forehead briefly, and when he looked back at Courtney, his poker face gave nothing away. Was he excited about the object she offered? If so, he was certainly playing it close to the chest. He cleared his throat. "Looks like an early twentieth century design, probably out of the Man o' War era. He won the Belmont Stakes in 1919."

TMI. "I don't know anything about that. The fellow at the tack shop extolled the virtues of this crop's flexibility. He said the leather was triple cured, so that it did its job in urging the horse forward but didn't impart a lasting sting." Courtney could feel Eric's eyes on her, but she was too nervous to meet his gaze. She rifled around the bottom of her purse, as though the crop had lost a screw.

"Let me see it." Eric reached for the crop.

Courtney handed it to him, strap first.

Eric reached back to her hand for the crop's handle. "First thing you should know, try to minimize contact with the actual crop. Body oils will deteriorate the leather, so always hand the crop to someone like you would offer a knife, handle first."

Courtney squeaked out an, "Okay, then what?"

"Then you're going to want to cover your palm with a piece of fabric. I'll use this linen cocktail napkin." He tucked the ends of the napkin between his fingers to keep it securely in place. "The fabric not only keeps body oils off the crop, but it adds a layer of protection."

"Like horsehair?" Courtney asked.

"Not as protective as horsehair, but at least not leather on bare skin." He looked at her from under his eyelashes as he smacked the crop on his palm.

Surely, he saw her shiver. "I hadn't thought about the logistics. I assumed a thong would be the clothing of choice."

•••

"A thong?" *All right, Miss Sexpot, two can play this game.* "What else have you 'assumed'?"

"Well," Courtney inched closer to him on the couch, "I figured there might be some conversation about how the thong wearer—shall I call her the thongee?—had been a bad girl." Courtney winked at him. He couldn't recall her ever winking before.

"Go on." Eric draped an arm over the back of the sofa, just inches from Courtney's shoulder.

"You see, the thongee knew she'd been pressing the limits of someone's patience."

Eric slapped the crop in his palm, again. "You know, this could really hurt."

Courtney licked her lips. She took several sips of bourbon, and then said, "I can only imagine how much it would sting … and titillate."

"Tell me more." Eric inched closer and began massaging Courtney's shoulder. She moaned, and he moved his hand to the back of her neck, kneading her scalp with his fingers.

"I figured they'd both be so turned on that after a few stings from the crop, he'd ease the thong out of the way and enter her from behind."

Eric tipped up his glass, finishing his drink. His breathing was ragged. He wanted to take one of Courtney's feet and pull it toward him so she'd be flat on the couch. Fortuitous for her that she wore pants because if she were in a skirt, he'd have her without further preamble. He didn't want to hit her with a riding crop, but he sure as hell wanted to make love to her. And damn if she wasn't ready. Eric ran a hand through his hair. He wanted to devour her, and when he pulled her into his arms, he saw desire in her eyes, as well as fear.

"Sure you're ready for this?" Eric asked.

"Uh, I thought I was." She chewed on her bottom lip. "Could we maybe order that pizza now?"

Eric chuckled. He moved away from her, rolled his shoulders and relaxed back into the sofa. "I was wondering when propriety would win out." He picked up his cell phone from the coffee table. "What do you like on your pizza?"

"You must think I'm a wuss."

Eric turned his body to her and took her hand. "Courtney, you're the most interesting woman I've ever met, but I don't know what you want from me, and I suspect you don't know, either."

"I've never had a relationship. I was the poster girl for geek until Helen got hold of me. "

"Geeks need love, too."

"Yeah, but this geek is hell-bent on sabotaging it." She inched away from him and watched his expression change as he dropped her hand. His smooth brow morphed to exclamation wrinkles between his eyes, and the corners of his mouth turned down. She hadn't meant to, but she'd just shut him out. Her heart plummeted to the pit of her stomach.

"You don't strike me as a woman who gives up easily."

"Not unless I hit a brick wall."

"Is that how you feel, like you've run into an immovable object?"

"No. Yes. I don't know." Tears welled in her eyes. "I think I should just go home."

Eric rose from the couch. "I'll take you home, but I want you to think about something." He pulled her to standing and took her chin in his hand. "Let go."

Chapter Nine

"After you told Eric you wanted to go home, you didn't say anything during the drive?" Helen's mouth gaped as she sat on Courtney's queen-size bed.

"Not a word." Courtney's voice cracked. "I'm an idiot. Everything was humming along beautifully. We were about to get the ball rolling, and then I just froze."

"Look at this logically, Court." Helen crossed her legs and held up one finger. "One, you're attracted to this guy." She stabbed her second finger in the air. "Two, this guy's attracted to you." She added her third finger and made the Girl Scout salute. "Three ... " She turned her hand palm up. "I don't see a three. Aside from you running so hot-and-cold, he probably thinks you have multiple personalities."

"Oh, God, I know. At any moment, demure Courtney morphs into weepy Courtney."

"And don't forget sexy Courtney."

"Yeah, but who's the real me?"

"They're all you, and they're all good."

"I don't think so. I'll match you finger for finger." Courtney stabbed one finger in the air. "One, I never used to get emotional on the job. From the first day I met Eric, I cared more about his vote than I should have. So what if he doesn't vote for higher taxes on tobacco? I can't convince everybody. Why is his vote so important? But no, I went and made his vote a crusade."

Courtney jumped off the bed and started pacing the room. "Two"—another finger went up—"this whole physical attraction thing is new to me. I ache when I'm not with him. It's like the worst kind of homesick." Courtney stuck finger number three in the air. "I had sex in a nice little personal compartment until I met Eric, and now I'm all befuddled. I think he's insanely hot, but whenever we get close, I chicken out. Why am I sabotaging myself?"

"Court, you're putting too much pressure on yourself worrying about trying to be some kind of sex goddess. Just be yourself!"

"I don't know." Courtney chewed on her lip. I've never met anyone so, so, special ... his sweetness, his dedication, his commitment to Travis. And when he kisses me, I want to die in his arms."

"Okay, that's important. Ponder that. And while you're in a contemplative mood, chew on this for a while—what scares you more ... failure or success?" Helen waggled her eyebrows. "In the meantime, I've got a deposition to take in the morning. I need some shut eye." She bounced off the bed. "But before we leave this discussion, are you really afraid that what Eric wants is kinky sex? Or is it possible that what you're really afraid of here is intimacy? Because when you look at the big picture, kinky sex is just a speck on the horizon, but intimacy is the whole shebang."

Courtney squeezed her eyes shut and blew out a huge breath. "I'm afraid I'll lose my edge, that all I've worked for will turn to mush because I'm blinded by a man."

"Sweetie, you gotta live a little! Stop trying to anticipate all the things that could happen and get out there and see what *does* happen, huh?" Helen nudged her thigh.

She let out a heavy sigh. "I know you're right. I guess. Okay, I'll try."

"Hey, you know what they say: Do or do not. There is no try."

She opened one eye and squinted at Helen. "Eleanor Roosevelt again?"

Her roommate shook her head. "Yoda." She ducked just in time to miss the throw pillow Courtney launched at her grinning face.

• • •

Eric drummed his pencil on his desk blotter. What did she want from him? Hell, what did he want from her? Friendship was out of the question. If they didn't end up lovers, they couldn't be friends. The tobacco issue had seen to that. And if she held out any hope of convincing him, she'd be sorely disappointed. No, they couldn't be friends, and after the upcoming vote on Valentine's Day, they might not make it as lovers either.

When he'd kissed her, the world stood still. All that mattered was Courtney in his arms. And it wasn't enough. He wanted to be inside her, to be the first man in her life, but he was at odds with her innocence versus her awkward attempts at dirty talk. Did that stuff really turn her on or did she think that's what he wanted to hear?

He'd tried to keep the evening light. He was afraid of becoming aroused and then going too fast if she wasn't ready. Maybe she'd stopped him because she was worried they'd get too rough—like he'd ever done that. But perhaps she thought he had. She probably assumed he took the riding crop out of the frame in his office so he could ride an occasional lobbyist or two. But his collection of what she thought was fantasy equipment was just that ... a collection, not all that different from the Teenage Mutant Ninja Turtles he collected growing up.

Would he want to spank Courtney? The thought of her naked across his knee maybe held a certain appeal, but seriously, he'd rather just be with her, holding hands in the park, eating popcorn at the movies, taking Travis to a ballgame. He shook his head, hoping to clear his confusion. This continuous loop was getting him nowhere.

If he were smart, he'd give Courtney some space. That way she could figure out what she wanted. And he could, too.

...

Courtney didn't hear from Eric for a week. Though she was busier than she'd ever been, he constantly invaded her thoughts. It was that kiss. Why did she torture herself, reliving his lips on hers, the sensuous way he'd eased his arm around her and pulled her close, the taste of him mingled with his scent of spice and woods after their day at Manassas. She shook her head, trying to clear the image of how sexy and dark his eyes were when their kiss ended, staring at each other, their breathing shallow with yearning.

Trying to forget about him, she threw herself into securing the last few votes she needed for the tobacco tax. It was going to be dangerously close. Commitments from senators in Arkansas and Oklahoma were solid, but Florida and South Carolina could go either way, and without Eric's vote, the bill was in serious jeopardy. But she wouldn't try to convince him again. He'd dug in his heels, and in her objective moments, which were few where he was concerned, she could even understand his point.

That afternoon, she heard Bill clipping down the hall in his Gucci loafers and waved him into her office when he rounded the corner. "What's your count?" he asked.

"I'm close. I'll visit with Arkansas and Oklahoma again today. Senator Flutie from Arkansas is hot on the pig farmers' bill, and he's been trying to trade votes with Virginia and North Carolina. He told Senator Morrison he'd support price election on tobacco if Morrison backed him on the pigs."

"Besides price election, what are Morrison's hot buttons?" Bill loosened his tie and took the chair opposite Courtney's desk.

"He likes the non-profit bill with the stipends for Special Olympics. That's a tough one because there are some organizations bundled with that bill that support lesbians and gays, and some of the more conservative senators won't support it. It's a shame because several of those non-profits are focused on bullying in schools." Courtney chewed on a fingernail, and then slapped her hand away. She almost had nails now, but the stress of this week had her reverting to old habits. "He could probably get a few price election votes from conservative senators if he voted against the non-profit bill, but I don't think he'd do that." Courtney couldn't help but smile—and sigh. "He's too principled."

"You like this guy?" Bill's eyebrows shot up.

Courtney sucked in her lips, wiping away her smile. "I was skeptical that all his do-goodness was for show, but he's for real. Yeah, I like him."

Bill nodded, shrewd eyes sizing her up. "Just be careful. Hook-ups like that can derail a career. If the media saw you two cozied up somewhere and Morrison ended up voting for the tobacco tax, his constituents would crucify him. He'd never get re-elected."

Her scalp prickled with the heat of embarrassment. She'd been so busy sabotaging any hope of intimacy with Eric, she hadn't considered either of their careers—another indication that her brain wasn't working on all cylinders. So, to get back to Bill's warning, a hook-up was probably a moot point. "Don't worry about that—on two counts. I doubt he'll change his vote on the tobacco tax, and I don't think I'll be seeing him again."

Bill pushed himself out of the chair, tightened his tie. "That's for the best. Want a recipe for disaster? Pair a lobbyist with a legislator." His cell phone chirped, and he answered it as he walked out of Courtney's office.

She stared at the door after he left. A dull ache settled in her heart. He was right.

• • •

In an effort to cheer Courtney up, Helen insisted they go to a Wizards basketball game on Sunday. The cheering fans might boost her spirits. Besides, she liked the draft beer and popcorn. She'd treat herself to a big pretzel, too.

The weather had returned to frozen tundra, which somehow made Courtney recall the unseasonal day she'd shared with Eric and Travis at Manassas. Scratch that. Someday, she might be able to look back and remember that outing with a smile, but now, the stab of pain brought tears to her eyes.

Courtney and Helen took the metro to Verizon Center. They were both bundled in more layers than they could count, and when they got to their seats in the nosebleed section, they were glad to find a few empty seats for piling their coats, vests, and scarves.

"I just lost twenty pounds," Helen said as she topped the pile with her wool cap.

Courtney laughed and reached in her purse for her binoculars. She liked watching the cheerleader routines before the game started. She flashed back to her high school football games. She'd played the tuba in the band. She remembered standing on the sidelines, watching the cheerleaders hug the football players after the game. What if she'd gone to school with Eric? He would have been one of the football players, probably team captain. But of course, she wasn't a cheerleader. She was the tuba nerd, and though she looked fashionable now on the outside, she was still a geek inside—the geek entranced with the football player, Eric.

Really, this obsession was getting old. She had to move on. "Let's get a pretzel." Courtney bounded out of her seat and grabbed Helen's elbow.

"Already?" Helen brushed off Courtney's hand. "Let me sit for a while. We can get a pretzel at the half. That way, it's like a reward."

"You need a reward to watch basketball?"

"I need a reward for braving this weather, and by half-time, I'll be thinking about bundling up again. The pretzel and a beer will keep my mind off the icicles I'll have to chip off my nose."

"Okay, I get that logic—sort of." Courtney sat down.

From the buzzer that signaled the game's start, the players shot back and forth on the court like racehorses. Maybe they were chilly and had to get their blood pumping, but whatever the reason, the scoreboard could barely keep up with the points ... on both sides. Courtney and Helen were out of their seats cheering with the rest of the hyped-up Washington crowd.

"And who said you can't get exercise as a spectator?" Helen asked. "My thighs are burning from all the up and down."

The two women started making their way to the concessions just before the bell sounded for first half. The Wizards were beating the Orlando Magic by two points.

Standing in the pretzel line while Helen got the beers, Courtney breathed in the mouth-watering aroma of pretzels, popcorn, and hot dogs, and then she felt a tug on her jean pocket. She turned, and her heart leapt when she looked down into Travis's brown eyes.

"Like my grill?" He smiled up at her, displaying new braces.

He must be here with Eric. Thud. "Very nice, and I like the red and black accents." *And I wish my stomach would stop churning.*

"They're my school colors. Cool, huh?"

She wanted to look around for Eric in the worst way, but she forced her eyes to stay focused on Travis. "I had braces, too, but not until I was in college. You're smart to get them while you're young. And they really are cool."

"Eric got 'em for me."

She heard his hello before she saw him. When she looked up, he smiled warmly. "I didn't know you were a basketball fan." He handed a Coke to Travis.

"Well, I figure I should support the home team." She smiled back.

"As a Floridian, I'm surprised you're not rooting for the Magic." His eyes grew dark and sexy as he looked at her.

Courtney's knees trembled. "No, I'm a Wizard through-and-through."

Travis poked her in the ribs. "Move up or somebody'll butt in line." He looked back and forth between Eric and Courtney. "You two are gettin' googly-eyed, and I don't wanna miss the second half. Can we get a pretzel, please?"

Eric laughed. "Sure, buddy."

Courtney was next in line, but Eric came forward and bought pretzels for her and Helen, as well as for Travis and himself. He handed her the pretzels and then motioned toward the condiment bar, where they squirted mustard into little plastic cups.

Eric tore off a piece of his pretzel and dunked it in the mustard, leaving a smudge of yellow on his lip when he took a bite. Courtney wanted to lick it off.

"Look who's here." Helen walked up and handed Courtney a beer.

Courtney ran her tongue over her lips, hoping to give Eric the hint about the glob of mustard. Instead, he simply stared at her lips.

"Oh, geez, you guys. Just kiss her and get it over with," Travis said. "The game's about to start."

"You've got a ..." Courtney reached up and touched Eric's lip. She swiped the mustard off and then licked her finger.

Eric grabbed her arm and pulled her close. Her beer sloshed over the rim.

She looked up into his gorgeous eyes.

With his lips close to hers, he murmured, "Lady, you're driving me crazy."

Just before their lips met, a flash blinded her, and she realized a photographer had just snapped them. She squinted at his press badge but was only able to read *Washington Tattler* at the top, not his name, before he scurried off into the crowd.

"I guess we'll be the talk of the town tomorrow," Eric said.

Courtney thought he looked remarkably calm … under the circumstances. "I'm sure the headline will be a shocker," Courtney said. She pressed a hand to her chest to still her racing heart. And then her brain kicked in. Again, she hadn't been firing on all cylinders. She'd just told her boss that Eric was *persona non grata* . She'd have to add "lack of credibility" to her growing list of character flaws. "If they call us an item, they'll be off base."

"That's a shame. I'd like to be your item."

Courtney sucked in her cheeks to suppress a smile. But it didn't work. She felt her eyes crinkle and her lips turned up. "What if they used the word 'romance'?"

"That's even better." He ran his tongue along his bottom lip.

Courtney wanted to leap back into his arms. She took a deep breath and blew it out. *All right, I let my heart rule my head, and you know what, I feel like shouting it to the world. Maybe being with Eric isn't the smartest decision, and yeah, I'm scared, but for once, I let my heart decide.* "Well, I guess we'll know what they call it when we read tomorrow's headlines."

Travis stepped between them and tugged on Eric's sleeve. "Come on. They blew the whistle. Let's go."

Eric ruffled Travis's shaggy mop of hair. "Okay, buddy." He looked at Courtney before he turned. "I'll call you."

Chapter Ten

The next morning, Courtney and Eric were front page above the fold in the *Washington Tattler*. Given that the photographer must have barely made the deadline, there was no story. Just a caption that read, "Is There Romance in the Air for Senator Morrison?" Courtney moaned when Helen poked her shoulder and slapped the paper on the kitchen counter.

"Nice work. Looks like you're getting ready to suck his face off." Helen chuckled.

Courtney hunched over the counter and clunked her head on the butcher block top. Ouch. "My boss is going to kill me."

"That's your first thought? Gee, if it were me I'd be thinking about how to parlay this story into a million-dollar book deal." Helen patted Courtney's back. "Look at the bright side, Champion will probably take you off the account. Then you won't have to worry about public exposure. You can just date Mr. Wonderful in the open."

Courtney straightened. She rubbed her brow. "I don't want to give up this account."

"In that case … "

"Yeah, yeah, I know. Goodbye, Eric Morrison." Courtney opened the refrigerator door and stared at the orange juice. She shut the door when her cell phone rang. Her first thought was that the caller was a reporter, but then she saw the i.d. It was Eric. Panic stricken, she dropped the phone, which bounced off the linoleum … in two pieces.

Still ringing, Helen retrieved it, snapped the cover back on, and answered. "Capitol Hill Escort Service; we aim to please."

Courtney could hear Eric laughing in the background. Great.

"She's here. Just a minute." Helen handed the phone to Courtney.

Courtney took a deep breath before answering. "Do you think they've tapped our phones?"

"Not unless you're a security risk."

"I may be."

"And I thought you couldn't get more interesting." Eric laughed, again.

"I can't believe you think this is funny." Courtney huffed.

"It's just a blip, Court."

She loved that he called her Court.

"Tell you what," he said, "we both need a break from this town. I have to go to Winston-Salem next weekend to check on my parents' house while they're in Europe. Why don't you escape with me?"

Helen, who'd had her ear pressed to Courtney's, nodded emphatically and mouthed, *yes!*

This getaway could be her last hurrah with Eric. She'd tell him they couldn't continue this ridiculous … whatever … and that they'd need to call it quits. But in the meantime, she'd have a lovely weekend with him, sort of for old time's sake, like there'd ever been any old times.

"Okay," Courtney said.

"Great. I'll have Lorena book us out on Friday afternoon, returning Sunday. Will that work?"

"Is she discreet?" Courtney chewed on her lip.

"She's more than discreet. She's worked for my family since before I was born. She knows all our secrets."

• • •

Lorena Eddington looked at her boss over the top of her glasses. "You think it's wise being seen with this woman, especially after this morning's story in that rag newspaper?" She picked up files from her inbox.

Eric nodded. "Nothing she can say will change my vote, so the only way being seen with her could negatively affect either of our careers is if I caved."

"Then it would look like she'd traded favors."

"Which neither of us would ever do."

"She's a smart woman. Doesn't she know you're dug in?"

"I don't think so. She still thinks she can convince me, which is why being seen with me is such a threat."

"When do you plan to clue her in?"

"Good question." Eric paced in front of Lorena's desk. "I would have already told her I wouldn't budge, but I don't want her to write me off."

"Because you want to continue to see her?"

"Exactly."

"You must really like her." Lorena pushed her glasses up her nose. "But is that fair? Aren't you leading her on?"

Eric slumped into the leather settee where visitors usually waited for appointments. "I want her to like me for who I am—apart from the tobacco issue."

"You're hoping if she gets to know the real you, she'll overlook the smoke coming out of your ears?" Lorena smiled then sat up a bit taller. "I've got it. Show her all the great things tobacco money has done for Winston-Salem, like the university, the airport, and the hospital."

"She's not easily swayed, Lorena." Eric scrubbed a hand over his eyes and pushed himself off the settee.

"And I thought no one could resist your charm." Lorena winked at him.

"Tell *her* that." Eric checked his watch. His two-thirty meeting had cancelled, which afforded him this rare leisure time, but he had to brush up on his three o'clock, due anytime now. As he walked into his office and closed the door, he wished his problems with Courtney were as simple as a difference in tobacco policy.

They'd be alone in his parents' big house this weekend, sleeping under the same roof. Though with sixty-four rooms and guest rooms in a separate wing, it could be more like being in adjoining counties—unless she was in his room.

Maybe they'd get to the crux of what they both needed. Eric gazed at the photos on his wall, stopping at the framed riding crop. When Courtney had seen it, they'd locked eyes. He thought about riding her lush bum, but he'd never use a crop . He could never hurt her.

Chapter Eleven

No direct flights from D.C. to Winston-Salem fit their schedule, so they had a brief stop in Charlotte to change planes. After consulting The Weather Channel, Courtney packed light. She took a couple of sweaters and a three-quarter length, all-weather coat for a possible light snow, though the temperatures were expected to hover in the low fifties for most of the weekend. Eric said it was a typical North Carolina winter, but he added that the weather in general was warmer than he'd remembered it growing up. No doubt global warming at work.

When they arrived in Winston-Salem, Eric picked up the car he kept at the airport while Courtney waited at baggage claim. He strode back into the terminal to take their bags while people did double takes. The Roark/Morrison family members were obviously like royalty in this town.

The short drive from the airport to the entrance of Roark Manor became five minutes longer as the evergreen-lined boulevard meandered through Roark property. "We're almost there," Eric said as they rounded a turn and a split-rail fence gave way to wrought iron gates. Eric stopped at the gate to punch in his code at the key pad.

Courtney stared in awe as the expansive estate came into view. "It's breathtaking," she said. Her eyes scanned from side-to-side to take it all in—two stories and broad as a football field, but it didn't overwhelm the landscape. Matching wings abutted the main house, creating a gentle "u" shape that hugged a circular driveway. The house seemed to grow out of the earth, like it had checked in with the majestic oaks and pines to get their acceptance before laying its foundation. A porch ran the full length of the first story, and Courtney imagined revelers decked out in finery and sipping mint juleps. But that would be in summertime. Today, they'd be clad in furs around a bonfire, drinking mulled wine. With a few icicles dangling from the covered porch, the house looked like a frosty, but approachable, queen.

"My great-grandfather built it in 1912," Eric said. "There's a full working farm on the property and a village with shops and restaurants. Granddad Roark built the village to serve the farm laborers and house staff. He also built a school and church. It was a true sustainable community and in many ways, still is."

Eric stopped the car in the circular drive at the front door.

"You said your parents are away. Will we be alone in the house?" Courtney hoped.

"Just you and me ... and the staff," Eric said.

"Staff? What is this, *Downton Abbey*?"

At that moment, the front door opened, and a gentleman who looked to be in his late fifties, bounded to the car. "Mister Eric, it's so good to see you!" The smile on his face was broad and genuine.

Mister Eric? This is Downton Abbey.

"Nice to be home, Randolph. May I introduce you to my friend, Courtney Larson? Courtney, this is Randolph Small. He manages the house." Eric handed Courtney's bag to Randolph.

"I joined the Roarks thirty years ago," Randolph said.

"And he's indispensable," Eric said.

Randolph beamed. Obviously, he and Eric were fond of each other.

Courtney stepped into the massive reception hall and inhaled a deep breath of lemon furniture polish, warmed by a crackling fire. The entire room gleamed with rich wood, from the inlaid parquet floors to the exquisite pipe organ and the enormous claw feet on the matching sofas that framed the fireplace. Double staircases led from each side of the fireplace to a second floor balcony that encircled the room.

"My parents were married in front of that fireplace," Eric said, nodding to the marble mantel and expansive hearth. "And in the old days when my great-grandparents lived here, they used to roll up the rugs and host huge parties for the villagers."

Randolph started up the stairs. He stopped and turned at the landing. "We set up the Truman room for Miss Larson."

"The Truman room, as in President Harry?" Courtney asked.

"Yes, he's our claim to fame ... the one president who slept in this house. He came to Winston-Salem for the dedication of the university."

"Which your family funded?"

Eric nodded and then pointed to an arched doorway to the right of the reception hall. "That's the library. Want to meet me there in a half-hour or so? Randolph will take you to your room. You can unpack and get comfortable."

Courtney felt she had stepped back in time, particularly when the grandfather clock chimed. The melodious sound echoed through the reception hall.

"Five o'clock," she said, "must mean it's time for sherry?"

Eric smiled wryly. "I prefer a local microbrew."

Courtney headed up the stairs, where Randolph motioned for her to follow him. She stopped to look back at Eric. "Do I dress for dinner?"

"I'm going to change into jeans and a sweater, so just get comfortable. We're not entertaining a president tonight." He turned to ascend the staircase on the opposite side of the fireplace.

No, but doesn't the vestal virgin count for something? As she watched him disappear into the opposite wing, she mused about their sleeping quarters being so far apart. She wished he'd just taken her bags to his room, but of course, he wasn't a man to make assumptions. And besides, there was the issue of propriety. She was reminded of Katherine Howard, fifth wife of Henry VIII, who ran through the corridors of Hampton Court, searching for

Henry to plead for mercy. Wait a minute, what did losing one's head have to do with losing one's virginity? Not much, she hoped.

• • •

Courtney unpacked in the Truman room, where ivory, dial telephones donned the bedside table and the elegant ladies' desk. The whole house dripped old money, but there was nothing ostentatious about it. The Morrisons didn't need to toot their horns. Everyone knew who they were. But it was more than that. This house exuded old world sophistication, and the way it was tucked into the land made Courtney feel embraced. This was a family home.

She sighed. Why had Eric brought her here? Was this the venue of a final confrontation on tobacco, or in the words of Helen, would this be the scene of her *cherry pop*? Talk about a lasting memory.

And where did you surrender your virginity, Courtney? What's that? Speak up, girl.

You were spending the weekend at the Morrison/Roark mansion in North Carolina?

That would be the Morrisons and Roarks of tobacco fame?

And aren't you a lobbyist for the opposition?

Shame on you, Courtney.

Yeah, shame on me. Courtney unpacked with a wicked smile. She laid out a pale pink cashmere sweater and her J. Crew lilac cords. Slipping off her traveling clothes, she shrugged into the soft sweater, belted her jeans with skinny leather, and bent over to fluff her hair. When she straightened and finger-crimped her hair, she spritzed it with her favorite crunchable spray, and then took ballet flats from a plastic bag. She liked the idea of being so much shorter than Eric. She could wrap her arms around his taut middle and tuck her head under his chin. She swept blush across her cheeks, dabbed on a thin layer of peppermint pink lip gloss and checked herself in the mirror. Yep, she looked ripe—and ready.

She found Eric in the dining room, sipping a beer as he leaned against a massive sideboard that looked like it had been fashioned from an ancient oak, complete with all the gnarls and knots. It was a modern juxtaposition to the Duncan Phyfe dining room table that sat twelve, but everything blended beautifully. Courtney had the feeling that no decorator had put this eclectic mix together. No, the impeccable taste of the residents had been at work. And Eric inherited that taste.

"Beer?" he asked. "I'm afraid the fall brews are all gone, and we won't have any new locals until spring, but I've got a great raspberry ale."

"Love one," Courtney said as she watched Eric pull open a drawer in the sideboard that turned out to be a mini cooler. "What's for dinner?" *I could go for flank of Eric.*

"Randolph's wife, Katherine, left us something in the warming oven. Honestly, I haven't looked." He hooked his finger in a "come hither," and turned to the doorway that led to the kitchen.

The first impression of the kitchen was its lack of color. Gleaming white. From cabinets and appliances to the white tile backsplashes, it looked like a place where a wedding banquet for hundreds of guests could be whipped up in a matter of hours. All the counter tops were stainless steel, and the huge appliances screamed utilitarian. "Wow, I feel like I'm in the kitchen of the Waldorf Astoria. It's so industrial."

"When this house was built, it was all about hygiene. My great-grandmother wanted a kitchen that could be hosed down. She was quite the innovator in germ warfare. She established her own dairy to protect her children from milk-borne illnesses, and she had specific instructions on how milkers' hands and cows' udders had to be washed with soap and water before milking."

"With the kind of money she had, I suppose she could do anything," Courtney said.

Eric dipped his head and looked at Courtney through his eyelashes. "It wasn't about money. She was driven by social reform. My family has great respect for farmers. There's nothing more vital than tilling the earth, and my great-grandmother wanted farmers to be successful. She tested new methods of crop rotation and soil analysis, all to support the individual farmer."

"Who was growing her tobacco, of course."

"Sure, there was tobacco, but that was just one of many crops. She wanted to make all the local farms self-sustaining. I wish you could have seen how hard these people worked, and my ancestors worked right alongside them. Clearing fields is back-breaking labor, and even the women dug out and moved rocks the size of buckets."

Courtney nodded. "Okay, I'm impressed."

"And I haven't even gotten into animal husbandry."

"Please, no sex talk before dinner." *Did I really say that?*

Eric laughed. "Okay, but it's fair game for dessert." He winked and then looked away, just in time to miss the red blush that Courtney felt creeping up her neck. "Anyway, this kitchen has seen its share of big events." He opened the warming oven and inhaled deeply. "Ah, I should have known Katherine would make one of my favorites. I hope you like meat loaf."

"Who doesn't?"

"Katherine makes it with ground beef, pork, and turkey. Sometimes she adds venison, but Mom hates it when Dad culls the deer. It's no wonder we get a bumper crop. She keeps two big barrels full of corn stocked for them." Eric removed a gravy boat covered in tin foil from the warming oven. "I see she's made her famous mushroom gravy to go with the meat loaf." He closed the oven and opened the refrigerator. "And there's a salad, so we're set."

Courtney suspected he'd always been coddled with good food.

As though he'd read her thoughts, Eric said, "Yep, I was a spoiled rich kid."

Randolph appeared in the doorway, his hat in hand. "Don't you believe it," he said to Courtney. "Eric slopped hogs with the rest of us."

• • •

Courtney woke on the memory foam mattress (good to know there were some concessions to modern comfort in this stately home) and replayed the previous evening in her head. The part where Eric lifted her off her feet to kiss her was on a continuous loop. She'd thought he was going to swing her into his arms and carry her up the staircase, *a la* Rhett Butler, but no, he'd just set her down and tapped her nose. She half expected him to pat her butt when she ascended the stairs, but of course, he was too much of a gentleman for that. She could feel his eyes on her, though, and she made the most of her slow climb with a bit of hip action.

Today, he would show her Old Salem and downtown Winston-Salem. She rolled out of bed, and after her morning toilette (in the modern bathroom, not with a bowl and pitcher), she dressed in a pair of gold cords, an argyle sweater in tones of brown and turquoise, and ankle boots with practical, two-inch heels. She piled her hair into a high ponytail and secured it with a leather barrette.

She didn't have to wander around too long downstairs to find Eric. She followed the aroma of freshly brewed coffee and found him in a sunny room behind the kitchen.

"Ready for a cup?" He proffered a coffee pot.

"Absolutely," Courtney said, picking up a china cup and saucer from the sideboard and extending it to Eric. "This is a gorgeous room, kind of like a greenhouse."

Palms and ferns lined the periphery of the room, which was surrounded by windows and French doors leading to an outside porch.

"As long as it's sunny outside, this room stays pretty warm, even in the dead of winter," Eric said. "Speaking of which, we're supposed to get an icy mix today."

"Will that mess up our sightseeing?" Courtney hoped not.

"The front isn't moving in until this afternoon, so we'll get an early start." He squinted out the window to the bright sunshine. "I made some bacon. Let's grab a couple of pieces, and I'll take you for a tour of the house." Eric motioned for Courtney to lead the way to the kitchen and then they traveled through the dining room to the reception hall.

Courtney munched on a piece of bacon. "This has to be the best bacon I've ever tasted."

"Local and organic," Eric said. "Our farm served as an early agricultural extension office in the last century, and my grandmother was influential in introducing humane slaughtering practices. We eat our pigs, but they have fine lives before they make it to the table. All our animals are free range, and most are grass fed." Eric took a bite of bacon. "As I mentioned before, this room," he swept his arms around the huge expanse, "was the site of many village parties in my great-grandmother's day. And the organ over there," he pointed to an enormous pipe organ, "was the entertainment. It has more than 2,500 pipes."

"Do you play?" Courtney licked her fingers. Noticing that Eric paid close attention, she made a bit of a show of it, sucking on her index finger.

"Uh, no." Eric cleared his throat. "Shall we go upstairs?" Eric led the way up the wrought iron balustrade to the second floor balcony. "This is basically one big circle, with two wings of bedrooms and baths. In an age when bedrooms didn't have *en suite* bathrooms, my great grandmother insisted on them because of the spread of disease."

Every bedroom they walked through had an accompanying sleeping porch.

"Looks like people were really fond of sleeping in the fresh air," Courtney said.

"They thought it would ward off tuberculosis, which was the great scourge when the house was built."

Courtney plumped a pillow on a white wicker chair. "I'm amazed that your family was so concerned about health, and yet they ignored the hazards of tobacco smoking." She bit her tongue, but she couldn't help the comment. *I mean, really, were these people delusional?*

Eric had been walking ahead of Courtney, through a sleeping porch to his parents' bedroom. He stopped and turned. "It was a different time, Courtney, and they really didn't know the damage tobacco could cause. Do you watch the series, *Mad Men?* They smoked like chimneys all day long. Even pregnant women smoked. The dangers weren't known."

"And today they are." Courtney felt a chill, and she set her coffee cup and saucer on the glass-topped nightstand next to Eric's parents' bed. She rubbed her arms. "There's no getting around the proven dangers of tobacco."

"I won't argue with you on that. The surgeon general's warning on every pack of cigarettes makes the hazards clear, but we're a nation of free will. What do you want, Courtney, for tobacco products to be illegal?" He set his cup next to hers and crossed his arms.

"Well, ultimately, I wouldn't oppose that. But for now, all I really want is to keep young people from starting the habit."

"Kids are going to test the boundaries. The appeal of smoking is that it makes them feel more grown up. Plus, for most of them, they know their parents wouldn't approve. Seems to me that the

Campaign for Tobacco-Free Kids is doing a good job of appealing to young people to think twice before they take up a nasty habit."

"Ah, so you'll admit it's nasty." Courtney stood up a bit taller, straightening her back in victory.

Eric threw up his hands. "Why do we always come back to this?"

"Because we're at an impasse?"

"It's more than that."

"Because you're a highly intelligent man, and I don't understand why you can't see the light?"

"Your perspective, but still, more than that."

Courtney's breathing hitched as Eric stepped closer to her. He took her hand. Did he feel her tremble? "Enlighten me," she whispered.

"Because it's keeping us apart, and we want to put it behind us."

When his hands moved to her waist, she wrapped her arms around his neck. And when he bent to kiss her, she savored his soft lips and gently probing tongue. Her fingers tickled the prickly hairs on Eric's neck. He shuddered and hugged her tighter. She nipped at his lower lip when they ended the kiss then stepped out of his embrace, keeping her hands on his chest.

"Tobacco? What's tobacco?" She smiled up at him.

"Don't even think the word."

"Okay, truce." No tobacco talk. She could stick to that rule. Although, truth be told, tobacco wasn't the only thing keeping them apart. His fantasies were also a dubious area. Would Eric bolt if he found out what she wanted from this man was a gentle touch and some old-fashioned romance?

• • •

As Eric considered what he'd show Courtney in his home-town; he didn't want to overload her with the Roark/Morrison legacy—though it was tough to avoid. Even without pointing out the landmarks, the Roark and Morrison names adorned so many big edifices that short of blindfolding Courtney through town, there was no way to sidestep them. Heading into downtown in Eric's Range Rover, Courtney remarked about the Roark Memorial Hospital and the Morrison Library, as well as the Adelaide Powell Roark Cancer Center, named after his great-grandmother.

"Is there a nook or cranny around here that your family *hasn't* touched?" She asked. While the statement itself reeked of sarcasm, her tone didn't. She laughed. "Anything ordinary, like Morrison's Dog Groomers or Roark Beauty Parlor?"

"I think there's an Eric's Laundromat on the north side, but I can't lay claim to it."

"Seriously, your family has had a huge impact on this area."

"We've been here since the Civil War, so our roots run deep."

"It's not just that you've settled here, it's the good you've done."

"We're not unique, Courtney. We just give back."

"You're being modest, Senator. There are many rich ... and greedy ... people in the world who wouldn't dream of parting with any of their money."

One side of Eric's mouth turned up in a small grin. He was accustomed to praise, but Courtney's kind words really bolstered his spirit. He took a deep breath. As he blew it out, he pointed out the window. "Well, enough of my family. I thought we'd spend some time roaming around the historic area, Old Salem."

Eric pulled into the Frank L. Horton Museum Center. "See, there are a few buildings with other people's names." He chuckled. "We'll stop here at the Center for our tickets, which will get us into the exhibit buildings."

They began their exploration of Old Salem at the Museum of Early Southern Decorative Arts. They joined a tour that had just begun, and while Eric wasn't surprised at Courtney's intense interest (it takes a lifelong learner to know one), he was impressed with her depth of knowledge about Southern furniture and crafts. She identified Charleston craftsmanship and a couple of the renowned portrait artists from the American Revolution.

Not to disturb the tour, Eric whispered in Courtney's ear as they moved through the exhibit to an eighteenth century dining room, "I didn't realize a Florida girl would know so much about the Deep South."

"I love history," Courtney said. "I once got lost in the Smithsonian, and they almost locked me in for the night."

"Wasn't there a book about that?" Eric asked.

Before Courtney could answer, the tour guide gave him a stern look and then went into her spiel about early tobacco plantations in the area. Not willing to re-visit a sore subject, Eric steered Courtney to a side exit.

"What, we're not going to finish the tour?" Courtney asked.

"I doubt there's anything she can tell you that you don't already know." Eric opened the exit door and peered into the overcast sky. "Besides, I don't want you to miss the shops in the village, and it doesn't look like the icy mix is going to hold off much longer." He took her hand, which warmed immediately in his, and began walking north on Old Salem's Main Street. Breathing deeply, he realized how good it felt to have Courtney here with him. As many times as he'd walked the village of Old Salem, he didn't remember another time that he'd had such a spring in his step.

"Hey, slow down," Courtney said, tugging on his arm and pointing to Timothy Vogler's Gunsmith Shop. "I don't want to miss anything."

And they didn't. From the shoemaker shop to the apothecary, they immersed themselves in life as it had been in the early 1800s. When the Moravian Church bell clanged the noon hour, they stopped at the 1816 Tavern for lunch.

The moment they walked through the heavy oak door, Courtney said, "Oh ... my ... God, it smells so good in here, like a chocolate chip cookie married beef stew, and they gave birth to bread pudding and chicken pot pie. I'm on olfactory overload."

"You have to try the sweet potato fries," Eric said.

"Gladly," Courtney replied, and then she proceeded to order the pot roast soup with spoon bread as well as peach cobbler for dessert.

A light drizzle began tapping on the mullioned windows of their upstairs dining room just as Eric took a bite of Courtney's peach cobbler. He leaned back in his chair and patted his stomach. "If I made a habit of finishing your food, I'd be the size of a sumo wrestler."

"No, you wouldn't. You'd worry it off."

"You think I'm a worrier?"

"I think you care deeply about your community and your constituents. You probably lie awake at night worrying about how you can do right by them."

"I do." He reached across the table and took Courtney's hand. "And I'm sure you're just as much of a worry wart."

"Totally." Courtney finished the last bite of cobbler.

Eric looked out the window where the drizzle had turned into sleet. "I guess we're holed up for a while. Want some coffee or tea?"

"I'd love some herbal tea."

• • •

They stayed in the tavern for another hour, waiting for the sleet to subside.

Walking back to Eric's car through the meadow behind the tavern, Eric wrapped his arm around Courtney's shoulder as they crossed the cobblestone street to the parking lot.

She looked up at him. "Thanks for bringing me here. I had a wonderful day."

"Me, too," he said, opening the car door for her, "and it's not over yet."

Eric drove just a few blocks north of Old Salem to the center of downtown Winston-Salem.

"Where to?" Courtney asked.

"I want to show you the Children's Museum. It's been my mother's favorite project for the past five years." Eric parked on Liberty Street, and they walked two short blocks through drizzle to the museum.

The woman at the welcome desk immediately recognized Eric and sprang from behind it to shake his hand. "Senator Morrison, I am so pleased to see you here. Your mom was just in this past week."

"Yeah, I understand she practically lives here. She told me not to miss the new bird's nest exhibit."

"Absolutely, it's a must," the gray-haired woman, whose name tag read "Clare Dunwoody," pointed down the hall. "It's in the garden, through those double doors. Since the weather's not great today, it's a bit wet out there for the kids. You'll have the place to yourselves. Climb away!"

"Now, I'm really curious," Courtney said as they headed to the double doors.

Once outside, an interactive, crocheted playscape greeted them. Suspended on cables, the structure loomed over a grassy plot.

"Meet the bird's nest," said Eric. "It's the world's first crocheted jungle gym, kind of a Baltimore Oriole's nest for humans."

"And it looks like we have it to ourselves," Courtney said. She climbed into one of the entrance holes. "Come on in. It's damp, but what the heck."

Eric followed her in, and the weight of two adults in the dynamic gourd collapsed them together. They rolled on the knitted floor like two marbles at the bottom of a bag. Eric took the opportunity to pull Courtney close. They laughed and hugged, their legs intertwined. Eric rolled Courtney on top of him, her hair loosed from its ponytail, tickling his face. He tugged on a strand, bringing her lips to his. "For most of my life, I haven't wanted girls to read too much into a kiss. This time, I don't want you to underestimate what's behind it."

He closed his lips on hers. Before he could nudge hers open with his tongue, she'd already started a slow explore, running her tongue inside his bottom lip. He moaned, deepening the kiss and pressing his hand into the small of her back.

"Mommy, there are grownups licking each other and rolling around in there!" A little girl's voice shrieked.

Eric and Courtney abruptly ended their kiss, juggled themselves to sitting and clamped their hands across their mouths so they wouldn't laugh out loud. Eric motioned for Courtney to exit through a hole on the opposite side of the bird's nest, hopefully away from the child and her mother. Eric eased himself out then turned to help Courtney. They both smoothed down their pants once they were standing and nonchalantly walked around the contraption and back to the double doors, avoiding eye contact with the little girl and her mother.

"Was it fun?" A woman's voice rang out.

Eric turned slowly and faced the woman, who didn't register that she knew him. "More fun than a barrel of monkeys."

They raced out of the Children's Museum, holding their sides and laughing all the way to Eric's car.

• • •

As Eric pulled out of the parking space, Courtney said, "What if that woman had recognized you, or worse, been a reporter?" Her heart beat wildly in her chest. She wasn't sure if it was from the run to the car or the near-miss from the spectators … or Eric's kiss.

"I can see the headline now, 'Senator Morrison Resorts to Childish Ploy for Votes.'"

"More like, 'Senator Morrison Regresses as Tobacco Vote Nears Senate Floor.'" Courtney winced. "Sorry, I promised not to bring up the 'T' word."

"Apology accepted."

Courtney couldn't believe she'd mentioned tobacco. She studied Eric's profile, intent on the road ahead. She may not have upset him, but she definitely broke the spell. What could she say to make up for her *faux pas*? Before he'd kissed her, he asked her not to underestimate his intent. What was his intent? "How about this headline, 'Self-Destructive Lobbyist Snags Senator in Love Nest.'"

Eric glanced briefly at Courtney. "I'm all for the love nest snag, but what makes you think you're self-destructive?"

Courtney looked out the window, just in time to catch the imposing Morrison Library on the way back to Eric's family estate. She'd never encountered a family that had invested more in their community. "Helen would say I can't leave well enough alone."

"We have the potential for better than 'well enough,' Courtney."

"Think so?"

"Hope so."

Chapter Twelve

While Eric showered, he thought long and hard about how Saturday night might proceed ... or unravel. What he really *wanted* was to take Courtney to his bedroom and become intimately acquainted with various luscious parts of her. Then he'd offer a post-coital dinner of wine, cheese, and French bread ... and some chocolate-dipped strawberries. They'd eat naked and then they'd make love again. Nope, he decided as the hot, pulsating water from the showerhead beat reality into his addled brain, he knew he'd have to shelve that dream. Before he could, in good conscience, make love to her, he needed to tell her once and for all that he would not vote for the tobacco tax. But they'd made a truce not to discuss tobacco this weekend, and if he brought it up, she'd probably launch into lobbyist mode and any hope for lovemaking would fly out the window.

He was in a catch-22—damned if he did and damned if he didn't. And this was about more than sex, much more. He was falling in love with Courtney, and one false move could ruin more than a roll in the hay. Sure, they could make love ... and then mosey back to D.C. where the shit would hit the fan when he voted against the tax. On the other hand, he could tell her tonight that his position was intractable, she'd rant and rave, and they'd fly back to D.C. looking out of opposite windows of the airplane. After a curt handshake, they'd say goodbye ... forever.

On the plus side, maybe her stance had softened. She seemed sympathetic to the plight of the farmers and impressed with his family's philanthropy, but how far did that go? Would she forgive him for voting against the bill that meant the world to her?

Well, he couldn't take her to his bed under false pretenses.

So, they'd go to one of his favorite restaurants in the village. Being in public would at least keep temptation at arm's length. He'd go light on the alcohol because there'd be nothing better than some heavy petting in the library when they got back to the house, and he didn't want to get carried away. He'd have to play it safe.

In a perfect world, they'd have a future beyond the vote. But this was not a perfect world. And even if she forgave him, they'd still need to come to terms with what they wanted from each other physically. Beyond the fantasies they both enjoyed—in their heads—could love survive?

• • •

Courtney soaked in the deep, claw-footed tub. She paid special attention to shaving her legs, even to the little hairs on her hot-pink painted toes. What did Eric have in store for tonight? She'd hoped he'd want to stay in because an evening curled up on the couch with him would be her idea of heaven, but he'd seemed a bit wired on the way home from downtown, like he had some energy he needed to expel. Shoot, he could expel it on her!

As much as she'd like to get down-and-dirty with him, though, she feared she'd disappoint him with her lack of experience. Aside from what she'd read in romance novels or conjured in her wild fantasies, she was a novice on the mechanics. (She flashed to a mental image in *Popular Mechanics* of inserting rod A into slot B.)

Truth be told, wild fantasies had nothing to do with true affection or closeness, and with him, sex was about more than just fitting their bodies together. It was about sharing something with him she'd never shared with anyone else. It was about becoming one.

Face it, Court, you're falling in love. She took a deep breath then sunk under the rising water in the tub. She squeezed her eyes shut and thought about how she'd need to be honest with Eric ... even if it meant losing him. But not tonight.

Tonight she just wanted to be in his arms.

• • •

The restaurant, Sanctuary, had formerly been a small brick home. It was tucked on a quiet street near the university, an area more residential than commercial. Courtney tried to mask her disappointment at not staying at Eric's house by chatting incessantly as they exited the car and walked up to the front door.

The restaurant owner, who Eric introduced as Michael, led them to a small room that looked to be a former bedroom. He pulled out a chair for Courtney. "You'll be the only party dining in this room tonight." Courtney caught his wink to Eric. Theirs was one of three tables, each set for two diners. "We have a couple of special items since you were last here, Senator, including rack of lamb and veal piccata." He handed menus to Eric and Courtney. "The wine list is on the table. I'll be back in a few minutes to take your selection."

"Just bring us something from Shelton's. Whatever white you like, Michael," Eric said.

"Shelton's?" Courtney asked as the owner left the room.

"It's a local winery, and if I remember correctly, you like white."

"I do like white, but I don't eat lamb or veal."

"I've seen you gobble bacon, so I know you're not a vegetarian."

"No, but those baby animals never had the chance to grow up. Ever since I saw lambs frolicking in a spring meadow and a PETA film about calves, I swore off them."

"Good for you." He reached for her hand. "I can vouch for the trout; it's top notch."

Goose bumps rose on Courtney's arm when Eric turned her palm over and stroked it with his other hand. He could keep that up ... forever.

"Uh, this restaurant seems excellent, but I was kind of hoping we'd stay in." She could feel the heat creep up her neck with her bold remark.

The side of Eric's mouth twitched. "The temptation was too great."

"Temptation meaning me?"

"Precisely."

Courtney tingled all over from the palm massage. She wanted his hands on her breasts. "Sometimes the most sensible move is to give in to temptation."

"Sensible? I don't think so, Courtney."

"If you don't mind my asking, what was this weekend about?"

"It was, is, a chance to get to know each other better."

She narrowed her eyes. "Did you think I'd soften my stance on you-know-what?"

"I believe I know where you stand."

"So, if you weren't, aren't, going to seduce me, I guess I'll have to take matters into my own hands." She eased her foot out of her suede pump and inched her toes under the hem of Eric's gray wool trousers.

"You're playing with fire, Courtney. I have my limits."

"And just what might those limits be?" Courtney smiled seductively as she ran her toes up and down Eric's calf and placed her hand on his thigh.

"Let's just say you're getting dangerously close." He grabbed her hand under the table, just as Michael returned with the wine.

"I think you'll like this Sauvignon Blanc." Michael seemed oblivious to the near miss he'd interrupted. "Who'd like to taste?"

"I'll let the lady do the honors," Eric said. He let go of her hand then removed reading glasses from his shirt pocket.

Courtney swirled the wine in the glass and took a sip. She noticed a slight flare in Eric's nostrils as he picked up the menu and buried his face in it. His breathing seemed deep, like he was trying to calm himself. Good.

• • •

Much as my dick's about to explode, I am not going to cave. Holy shit, I need a drink! Eric picked up his wine glass and almost emptied it in one gulp. He'd told himself he needed to keep his wits about him, but right now, he wanted the calming effects of a little alcohol.

"Would you like me to order for us?" He continued to peruse the menu, not daring to look at Courtney. She was probably licking her lips, and he didn't need that image.

"Sure. Want to start with oysters? I've never tested their aphrodisiac qualities."

Eric lowered the menu just far enough to reveal his eyes. He peered at her for a long moment before answering. "Not a good idea."

"Mind if I ask why you're being so coy?"

"Men aren't coy."

"Okay, then, evasive?"

He set the menu down. "Courtney, I think we should wait."

"Why?"

"I don't take your virginity lightly."

"Why don't you let me worry about that?" She sighed. "You can't imagine what it's like to be a twenty-seven-year-old virgin. It's embarrassing."

"Wait a minute, now I'm starting to feel like the means to an end." Eric laughed.

Courtney touched his hand lightly. "No, you're much more than that, and if I have to admit it, I appreciate your concern. But I'm beginning to understand what sexual frustration is."

Out of Eric's peripheral vision, he saw Michael approaching.

"Are you ready to order? Would you like to start with some *bruschetta*?" Michael asked.

"Is it loaded with garlic?" Eric swiped a finger across his eyebrow, which was moist with perspiration. Courtney was sexually frustrated and embarrassed, but she'd said something else that truly jolted his heart. She'd said he was 'much more' than a means to an end. Maybe she really cared about him. Now, more than ever, he had to make sure they didn't end up in the sack.

"Do you want it to be?" Michael asked.

"Yes, absolutely. I want it to ooze out of my pores."

Both Courtney and Michael's eyes grew wide.

"All right, then," Michael said, "I'll get going on that while you decide on the rest of the meal." Michael gave Eric a quick nod and left the room.

"Do you think I'm a vampire? Because if you're trying to put me off with garlic, I'll eat as much as you. We'll neutralize each other."

Eric raked his fingers through his hair. "I should have known you'd come up with a cogent counter."

"Hey, counselor, no one said we weren't equally matched."

"Will you excuse me for a moment?" Eric pushed back from the table, and though he was in no shape to stand up, he kept his napkin strategically placed in front of him as he pushed his chair back under the table and quickly turned to leave the room. He needed to splash water on his face … and maybe down his pants. When he closed the one-man bathroom door, he gripped the sink and stared at himself in the mirror. Courtney was coming on to him like there was no tomorrow. He'd need to turn the tide to dissuade her.

Think. Think. Think. Aha!

He cupped his hands with water, splashed his face, and dried off with paper towels as his plan took root.

Returning to the dining room via the kitchen, he completed the dinner order in conversation with the chef, ordering carrot soup and trout *meuniere*. The pungent smell of garlic made his eyes water when the *bruschetta* reached their table. The chef must have minced every garlic bulb within a hundred mile radius of Winston-Salem.

"Save some for me," he said to Courtney, who had a large square of *bruschetta* poised in her hand.

"Don't worry. We'd have to take separate cars if only one of us ate this." Courtney returned the *bruschetta* to her plate and fanned it toward Eric.

Eric sat down and reached for a slice. "If we went somewhere else after dinner, we'd clear the room." He took a bite.

Courtney laughed, her nose crinkling in the process.

"Listen," Eric said, weighing his words carefully, "there's nothing I want more than to make love to you, but I want it to be right." *Here comes the zinger.* "I don't have any of my accoutrements here in Winston-Salem, and I'm sure you'd enjoy the … event … more with the addition of some toys."

Eric smiled inside as all color drained from Courtney's face. Her posture stiffened and one hand flew to her neck to fiddle with a little diamond heart on a gold chain. So much for her bravado. "Well, that's not entirely necessary." Her voice cracked on 'necessary.'

"But it's your first time, and I want it to be all you expect."

She blinked … repeatedly.

"Let's wait until we get back to Washington." Eric reached across the table and took her hand. He'd bought himself some time, albeit with a lie that he'd have to back pedal out of later. But at least he wouldn't take her under false pretenses, and if she bolted after the vote, he wouldn't feel like a heel for stealing her virginity. Also, this was all so new for her. Maybe she'd gotten ahead of herself with the sexual innuendos. Maybe underneath her bravado, all she wanted was his vote. His heart sunk, but only momentarily. He didn't want to believe that, but could it have something to do with why she always pulled away?

For now, he'd be content with this small victory. Her first time should be with someone she really cared about. Eventually, he hoped that would be him.

• • •

Well, I royally botched that up. Deep in contemplation, Courtney chewed on her bottom lip. *What is Eric's modus operandi? Why is he so reluctant to go to bed with me?* She appreciated his concern about her virginity, truly she did. It warmed her heart. But her girly bits had other ideas, and darned if she wasn't ready to become a woman in the true sense. As each day dawned, she inched closer to competing in the Guinness Book of World Records as "Oldest Living Virgin." But it was deeper than losing her virginity. She respected this man, so while the lust factor was high, there was so much more to Senator Eric Morrison. She was even starting to understand his stance on tobacco, and wasn't *that* a paradigm shift? Oh, well, it looked like lovemaking was off the table for the evening, and maybe that was for the best. At some point, she'd need to tell him that the sex toys were unnecessary. Would that be the death knell for a relationship? She shrugged mentally, hoping there was no outward sign. Then with a heavy heart, she bit into the pungent *bruschetta* .

Chapter Thirteen

Valentine's Day couldn't come fast enough for Courtney, and it wasn't tied to the anticipation of a bouquet of roses or a huge box of chocolates. Nope. This Valentine's Day Courtney would know if the campaign she'd devoted so much of her time and energy to these past few months would benefit the lives of vulnerable youth ... or not.

Since she and Eric had returned from Winston-Salem, they'd had little time to see each other, which gave Courtney more time to consider her future. And she was quite sure she wanted Eric in it. He'd invited her for lunch at the Courtyard Café at the National Portrait Gallery, and with the vote just four days away, this might be her last opportunity to set the record straight ... before he cast his vote.

For once, Courtney arrived early—an attempt to calm herself for the revelation she'd spring on Eric. The Courtyard Café was one of her favorite spots in D.C. Housed in the Robert and Arlene Kogod Courtyard, it was a magnificent space under a glass canopy, and she'd attended a number of fundraising events here. But today, only a handful of patrons sat at the linen clad tables, sipping their illy coffee or glasses of wine. She and Eric would have plenty of privacy.

Suddenly, what had been nervous jitters in her stomach turned to churning waves. Instead of eating, they should stroll the museum first. Besides, she wasn't sure she could eat now anyway. She scooted back to the museum entrance to wait for Eric there.

He bounded up the steps of the Greek revival building, the collar of his overcoat turned up against today's gale force winds. She waved through the glass entrance doors, marveling at how handsome he was.

"Wow, you arrived before me. That's a first." He kissed her quickly on the cheek.

Courtney chose not to comment on why she'd gotten there early. "I love this place, and it's been ages since I wandered through the collections. I thought we might go upstairs before lunch. They've added a few new portraits to the "Struggle for Justice" permanent exhibit."

"Is that how you see your job, as a struggle for justice?" He half smiled.

"My stance isn't about justice, it's about personal responsibility." Courtney took a deep breath. "And that's what I want to talk about." She pointed to the broad marble staircase. "Let's go upstairs first."

Entering the exhibit, Courtney picked up a flyer about the portraits in the "Struggle for Justice," all of whom were major cultural and political figures—from key nineteenth century historical figures to contemporary leaders—who struggled to achieve civil rights for disenfranchised or marginalized groups. She led the way down a long corridor, stopping at the portrait of United Farm Workers organizer César Chávez.

"Interesting you should stop here." Eric nodded to the portrait. "He's one of my heroes."

"I'm not surprised." Courtney reached for his hand. "Chavez devoted his life to the conditions of farmers, and that's what you do for your constituents."

"I certainly try."

Courtney took Eric's other hand, so they stood facing each other in front of the portrait. "I know your heart is in the right place, Eric, and you need to know that the way I feel about you has nothing to do with how you're going to vote on the tobacco tax." She squeezed his hands. "There, I said it."

Next thing she knew, Eric had pulled her into his arms. He breathed into her hair, that wonderful warm breath of his. She inhaled his glorious spicy scent as he said, "Courtney Larson, you're the best thing that ever happened to me."

• • •

Courtney panicked when her phone chirped and a text from Eric popped up, congratulating her on the vote and saying he was on his way to her apartment. A mixture of excitement and dread gripped her when she heard the knock on the door. He'd voted against the tax, of course, and in an odd way, she was proud of him for his stand. She froze for a moment. Now that the vote had been decided, she'd have to come clean about the kind of relationship she needed. But in this moment, all she wanted was to be in his arms.

She flung the door open and then skidded into him on the icy stoop. He lost his footing, and they toppled together onto the sidewalk. Arms and legs tangled, they rolled, and then came to an abrupt stop at the boxwood hedge lining the walk. Courtney sat up, laughing. Eric bounded to his feet and helped her up.

"I guess you're not mad at me," he said.

"Mad? Did you think I'd be mad?"

"I wasn't sure, but since your side won," he smiled, "I'm the one who should be licking my wounds."

"Are you licking your wounds?"

Eric pulled Courtney into his arms. He rested his chin on her head. "Oddly, I'm relieved. I felt duty bound to support my constituents, but the vote went the right way."

Courtney looked up at him. "Seriously?"

"Yeah. And I want you to know that your campaign did have an impact on me. I'm going to crack down on growers who are spiking up nicotine in tobacco, and I'm going to try to get incentives for growers to begin planting hemp and other environmentally-friendly crops. I truly believe it's the best option for my constituents' long-term survival. I don't have much influence in the North Carolina General Assembly, but I'll encourage everyone I know in state office to fund tobacco prevention and cessation programs. It won't happen overnight, but I'm committed to making changes."

"That's quite a confession, Senator."

"It's nothing compared to what's coming."

"What, now you're going to tell me that you have a wife and three children holed up in a Georgetown townhouse?" Courtney's heart raced. She was joking, but her tendency to prepare for bad news got the best of her.

"Of course not." He tucked her head back under his chin and caressed her neck. "I'm going to tell you what I really want. I just hope you want the same thing."

Courtney stiffened in his arms. Would this be the end of her hopes and dreams? Had he waited for this vulnerable moment with her high on the vote's victory to plead his case for BDSM? Had all his gentility been merely a ploy to get to this moment of truth? She hugged him tighter, wanting to prolong this last embrace before he found out she wasn't even close to the woman of his erotic dreams. She was a complete fraud. Well, she'd kept up the ruse as long as possible. Better face the inevitable.

Eric cleared his throat. "I'm in love with you, Courtney. I love you."

"What?"

"You heard me. I love you, and I want you, whenever you're ready to take the next step."

When Courtney opened her mouth, her teeth started chattering, but she managed to say, "I love you, too."

Eric laughed and hugged her tightly. "What say we continue this discussion inside?" He helped her up and they entered Courtney's townhouse. Just as she closed the door, it sprang open again. Helen bolted inside rubbing her arms from the cold, before she even noticed Eric and Courtney. When she saw them, she jumped, and then she looked closely at their expressions. "Uh, did I catch you two in the middle of something?" She held up a hand. "Wait, don't even tell me. I haven't been laid in so long, I don't think my heart could stand it. Just know that I'm happy for you two." She looked back and forth at them again. "Oh, God, you probably want to be alone, and here I show up like a bad penny."

"Actually, Helen, we were just leaving." Courtney glanced at Eric.

Eric smiled. "Yeah, we're heading back to my place."

"I'll just throw a couple of things in my overnight bag." Courtney turned and ran up the stairs.

•••

For two people who made a living through their powers of persuasion, they both seemed unable to utter a word on the drive to Eric's apartment. Courtney's heart was bursting with Eric's declaration of love, but they still hadn't settled the sex toys issue. She patted her overnight bag, which held her toothbrush, makeup, and a cute peach-colored teddy that Helen had given her in anticipation of this day. She hoped it would stand up to battle scars. She shivered.

"Cold?" Eric asked as he turned into his parking garage.

"No, just contemplating."

"People don't usually shiver when they're contemplating. What's up?" He looked at her briefly before heading up the ramp.

"I was just wondering how important those riding crops are to your, uh, enjoyment?"

"I've only used them on rare occasions when I have a particularly stubborn filly." Eric looked like he was stifling a grin. Courtney couldn't find the humor. Wait, did he say 'filly?'

"I wasn't talking about your enjoyment of horses."

"Oh, you mean the use of a riding crop as a sexual accoutrement?" Eric rubbed his chin. "Don't believe I've ever done anything like that."

"What? You don't want someone who's into whips and chains?"

Eric turned off the ignition and angled toward Courtney. "Court, I want you. If you feel compelled to use some props, I'll be willing to give them a try because I love you. But my collection of riding crops is just that—a collection."

"Wait a minute, what about that talk in Winston-Salem about you not having your toys with you?"

"That was to put you off. I didn't want to take you to bed under false pretenses, and I thought that if we made love before the vote, you'd think I was taking advantage of you."

Courtney undid her seat belt and slid onto his bucket seat. "Eric Morrison, you are one hell of a guy." She took his face in her hands and kissed him soundly.

When they finally came up for breath, Eric said, "What say we go inside?"

"Beat you there."

They were at the door of Eric's apartment in a record two minutes. Both breathless, they laughed as Eric fumbled with his key.

Once inside, Courtney said, "I've been wondering about the color scheme in your bedroom, Senator. Could I take a peek?"

"I thought you'd never ask."

The next thing Courtney knew, she was being led by hand down the hall. When they reached Eric's room, she glanced up at him before stepping through the door. The small muscle in his jaw began to tick as he walked her to the bed. He flicked on the bedside lamp, opened the drawer of the nightstand, and retrieved a condom. Courtney's heart beat in her ears.

Then he met her eyes, and any doubt floated out of the room. This was the moment she'd been waiting for. She took a deep breath.

• • •

Eric reached for Courtney's belt and pulled her to him. "I won't hurt you, Courtney. I won't ever hurt you." As he unbuckled her belt, unzipped her skirt, and slid it down her hips, he felt her relax under his touch.

"With every fiber of my being, I know that." She smiled. "And I'm a quick study."

He threw off his sweater. "Okay then, what're we waiting for?"

He worked on the little pearl buttons of her blouse while she pulled his shirt out of his pants. Slowly, they peeled each other's clothes off until Eric stood in boxers and Courtney faced him in a peach-colored lace bra and matching panties.

Eric traced his thumbs along the top of Courtney's push-up bra and then rubbed her nipples through the lace. She moaned, and that was the precise cue he needed. He swept the comforter off the bed, but before he could take her into his arms, she pulled down the top sheet and leaped in.

Sliding in beside her, he touched her cheek and then kissed her—a deep, wild kiss that intertwined their tongues in a dance he desperately wanted their bodies to do. While they kissed, he unhooked her bra and slipped off her panties.

He pulled her on top of him and stroked her back, pressing her breasts into his chest, heart-to-heart. He moved his hands down to her buttocks, spreading his fingers wide and cupping her there. Moving her hips in sensuous circles against his cock, he nibbled on her bottom lip. Then he flipped her over so he was on top … and he started moving down her luscious body.

"Where are you going?" She asked.

"Where do you think I'm going?" He took her breast in his mouth.

She moaned. "Just don't stop."

When he moved down to her womanhood, she arched her back. His fingers found her sensitive bud first, and then he closed his mouth on her. She bucked underneath him and moaned. He sensed her mounting pleasure and intended to finish her, but she had other ideas.

She put her hands on his temples. "I want to come with you inside me."

He smiled up at her, and then moved alongside her on the bed, turning her back to his chest. Reaching back to the nightstand, he took the condom, tore open the package with his teeth, and smoothed it down his erect shaft.

He ran his hand down the smooth porcelain of her back, and then lifted her leg high in the air. He positioned himself slowly, and then penetrated her sheath from behind.

She gasped.

"Hurt?" He asked.

"No, don't stop."

He grasped her knee so that she was splayed wide, and he cupped her mound, his fingers dancing across her wet bud, which he pleasured to the point of no return. He felt her climax begin to pulse before she gave into it, and when she did, her entire body jerked with the spasms of her delight, sending him over the edge. He exploded into her, riding the wave of his release until it finally subsided, and they collapsed together. Eric wrapped his arms tightly around her and breathed into her hair.

• • •

They stayed spooned, damp skin to hot damp skin ... and speechless ... until their breathing returned to normal.

"Oh, God, I almost forgot. It's Valentine's Day," Eric said.

"I think I got my present." Courtney snuggled her butt tighter against Eric's shaft, which answered with a nudge.

"And you might get it, again."

"Might?" Another nudge pushed against her. "You're getting persistent, Senator."

"Courtney, this is just the beginning of my persistence."

"Yeah? How long can you keep it up?"

Eric laughed. "Are you talking about my hard-on?"

"I'm talking about your heart." Courtney's own heart raced as she waited for Eric's response.

"How does forever sound?"

"Good. Very, very good."

About the Author

Susan Blexrud divides her time between Orlando, Florida and Asheville, North Carolina where she leads two book clubs, advocates for gay youth, writes a monthly column for All Souls Cathedral, quilts, watches birds, and maintains a public relations consultancy. She's the married mother of two grown children, and her constant writing companions are a Chihuahua named Baby and a cockatiel named Romeo. *Valentine Vote* is her third novel for Crimson Romance.

More from This Author
(From *His Fantasy Maid* by Susan Blexrud)

Amy

If I believed the adage, "you are what you do," my self-concept would be in the toilet, so to speak. I clean houses in a bikini or French maid get-up, client's choice, which contributes little to making the world a better place. As a result, my adage is, "you are what you become," because I'm becoming a doctor.

But today, I'm Amy Maitland, fantasy maid.

My best friend and fellow medical resident, Ellen, knows about my undercover life working for Fantasy Maids, but she's the only one. If word got out at the College of Medicine, I'd be the laughingstock of the University of Central Florida. My five brothers know I work as a housemaid, which they respect as good, honest labor, but they don't know the fantasy aspect. Protective (and controlling) men that they are, they'd lock me up.

That said, it's not the worst job in the world. I've been a fantasy maid for almost two years; so far, none of my clients has tried to assault me. But it's always a possibility, considering Florida's propensity for perverts. The company (i.e. Rex, the owner and a part-time secretary) arms us with pepper spray and an emergency hotline number (Rex's cell phone), and they screen the customers to make sure no one's a registered sex offender. They also arrange our appointments and Rex is good about following up — within four or five days — to make sure we survived the gig.

Still, being alone with a strange guy in his apartment is enough to get anyone's adrenalin pumping and I never go into a new situation without first sending up a prayer. I always let Ellen know where I'm going and I carry a rosary, even though I'm not

Catholic. A childhood friend gave me a strand of the rose-colored beads for Christmas one year, and they've been my protector ever since.

Today, I'm heading to a condominium in stylish Winter Park, just north of Orlando. The address alone is comforting. It's just off Park Avenue in a nice neighborhood next door to a church. But I remind myself Ted Bundy lived in a nice neighborhood. Let's face it: serial killers *can* look like the boy next door.

My old, white Honda sputters into the church parking lot adjacent to the condominium complex without any signs of cardiac arrest (this I take as a good omen). The Rambling Waters sign on the wrought iron gate looks welcoming.

I turn off the ignition and my ancient car heaves a sigh. Grabbing my backpack with my stash of costumes, I hop out of my car and punch in the security code at the entrance gate. It creaks open like the sound at the beginning of Michael Jackson's Thriller, which my brother Matt plays ad nauseam around Halloween.

As I enter the property, I notice a network of ponds meandering around the buildings. I'm sure the landscape architect intended them to be beautiful, but all I see is a maintenance nightmare — all that algae to eradicate. I shake my head. I've been cleaning too long.

I nod to an elderly couple walking their white miniature poodle. The dog is decked out in a purple vest and ear bows and looks slightly embarrassed. Good to know I'm not the only one who wears ridiculous outfits.

"Can we help you find something, dear?" the woman inquires. Could it be because I'm standing here with the address in one hand and a blank stare on my face?

We're supposed to look inconspicuous when we arrive at a job so the casual witness doesn't get wigged out by a neighbor's proclivities. To that end, I'm dressed in my usual jeans and t-shirt. Would she call me dear if she saw me in uniform?

My appointment is for six P.M. and I'm already a few minutes late. I count seven buildings on the property, with no visible numbers. Gratefully, I say, "Thank you. I'm looking for unit Five B."

The woman elbows her companion. "Oh, that's where that nice young lawyer lives. What's his name, Harold?"

Harold shrugs and the woman pulls her poodle away from the geranium it's been nibbling on. She cups one hand around her mouth and points to Harold with the other. "He's not very observant." She rolls her eyes. "Building Five is just to the right of the pool, which is straight ahead."

"Thanks." I head in the direction she indicates. My sandals crunch as pavement gives way to gravel. I look down to find strategically-placed stepping stones in the shape of turtles. Strategically placed for Big Foot, that is. The stones are way too far apart for my five-foot-three leg span. I essentially hurtle from turtle to turtle, using my backpack for ballast. I'm working up a sweat in the May humidity.

Behind me the woman calls out, "Spending the night?"

It's none of her business either way, but when you reach a certain age, you don't mince words. I find that endearing. It's one of the reasons I'm leaning toward a specialty in geriatrics. I stifle a smile and leap on like I don't hear her.

I count twenty turtles by the time I find Five B, which is on the second floor. I squint into the partly cloudy sky and cross myself before I start up the steps to indulge the imagination of my latest employer. My sandals slap the stairs; the flat surface is comforting after the series of round turtle backs.

My nerves always wait until the last possible moment to go bonkers and, as I'm standing at the door poised to rap, my heart begins to pound so loudly I'm not sure I even need to knock. Rex promotes his fantasy maids as being "doe-eyed and dewy" when he talks with potential clients — "doe-eyed and dewy" being the equivalent of virginally innocent. Today, though, between rushing to get here, the turtle stepping stones, and the flight of stairs, I'm more drenched than dewy, which is not exactly the sexy image I'm supposed to project. Still, for better or worse, this is Florida where heat and humidity go hand in hand, meaning that if you exert yourself at all, "drenched" is to be expected. It must be ninety degrees. I dab at my face with my t-shirt then fan my hands under my arms to get a breeze going. I hope my deodorant holds up.

Okay, show time.

As my fingers reach for the claddagh knocker on the front door, I spot the doorbell and opt for that instead. The chime rings the theme from *Doctor Zhivago*. As it happens, my mom's favorite movie, God rest her soul. I'm caught off-guard and tears well up. I'm swiping at my eyes when the door opens.

The guy across the threshold presses a finger to his lips and pulls me into the condominium. He sort of props me next to the wall. "You don't have a cold, do you? If you do, I want a discount." He backs away and eyes me up and down then he grins. "Good old Claudia would shit a brick if she saw you."

"I take it I won't be meeting good old Claudia?" I shiver from the blast of air conditioning, though it's welcome relief.

"Hell, no, she's the fiancée ... and my sister. Stay right here. Don't move." He takes off down a hall.

"Uh, okay." Wherever this is going, all I can think is how grateful I am for the cool air. I rub my arms and glance around the uncluttered, tasteful living room. It's immaculately decorated in beige and chocolate brown, strong masculine colors. I can't imagine what I'm going to clean.

As I'm sizing up the job, another guy emerges from the hallway. One towel wraps around his tight-as-a-drum middle as he dries his hair with another. My jaw drops. I almost have to push it closed. Six feet, wavy dark brown hair, and broad shoulders ...

my dream formula. My belly tightens and I get a little twinge ... below my umbilicus.

"Whoa, pardon me," he says as he tosses his hair towel to his friend and tightens the one around his waist. "I didn't know we were expecting company."

"Surprise!" his friend bellows, clapping Mr. Gorgeous on the back. "She's an early bachelor party gift. Your groomsmen, yours truly included, decided to loosen you up a bit before we head to the strip club. May I introduce your fantasy maid?"

Oh, no, my least favorite client (aside from a rapist, of course) is the fellow who gets a fantasy maid as a gift. There's inevitably time wasted while everyone has a good laugh. Well, not everyone laughs. The tricksters do. The trickee typically hems and haws and turns ten shades of red. But the tricksters always prevail. They've paid for the service and by God they're going to ensure that some cleaning gets done.

This is where I ask, "Do you have a room where I can change and would you like the bikini or the French maid outfit?" Today I'm kind of wishing I'd brought another outfit to suggest, as in one that might fulfill my own fantasies where this particular client is concerned. Although, the towel he's wearing with nothing under it is working pretty well — if I let it, which ... I really shouldn't. Besides, after working up a sweat outside, I've got goose bumps from the air conditioning that make me wish guys fantasized about fur-clad Eskimos cleaning their apartments.

Of course, maybe my goose pimples are a sign of something else, like the sight of this yummy man.

"Look, Miss ... what's your name?" This from Mr. Gorgeous, who looks my age or a few years older. He extends one hand for a handshake, holding fast to his towel with the other. I wonder if he's ticklish.

I place my hand in his. Warm fingers wrap around mine. Very nice. "I'm Amy, your fantasy maid." My voice is at least an octave higher than usual. His eyes grow wide. I guess he wasn't expecting me to squeak. Clearing my throat, I launch into my shtick. "I'm here for two hours to provide anything you need in the way of cleaning. I even do windows." I display a toothy grin. What is wrong with me?

"Well, I'm Jake. And while I appreciate the generosity of my groomsmen," he looks at his friend and mock-growls, "you don't need to stick around to do my cleaning." He smiles and I swear his eyes twinkle.

I melt. I'm staring into his green (my favorite color) eyes and I have a compelling urge to brush the hair off his brow and step closer. If his embrace is as warm as his handshake ... stop it. Also, he's just had a shower. He smells like sandalwood. I want to lick him. I shake my head ... and my thoughts. Back to work. As Rex says in our Fantasy Maid Manual, "When the client is reluctant, press on ... with finesse."

"So, French maid or bikini?"

"I'd go for the bikini," his friend pipes in. "And if you take her up on the windows, I'll get the ladder. Bet the view is great."

Yuck! But I act professional, even in this most unprofessional situation. "Just so you know the rules, there's no touching." As I look back at Jake, I'm thinking I should have kept my mouth shut. I want to run my hands down that washboard stomach. Stop that. "I clean and you're welcome to watch. This is a cleaning service, not an escort service."

"That's good to know," Jake says. I see the wheels turning in that beautiful head of his. He seems to be softening. He shrugs. Bingo. "Tell you what, my dishwasher needs to be unloaded and you can make my bed and straighten up in the bedroom. Do you iron?"

"Yes, sir, I do. In fact, I love to iron." Phew, a task. Nothing like a task to tamp down the hormones.

"Great, there are a few shirts hanging above the dryer in the laundry room. The board's in a narrow closet and the iron is in the cabinet above the sink. And please don't call me sir."

I nod. This guy is organized. It's a great combination, gorgeous and organized. "So, if you'll just show me where I can change?"

His friend (still don't know his name, but the one who's doing this for *his sister's* fiancé?) rubs his hands together. "Oh, boy."

"It's not necessary for you to change," Jake says. "Just do the tasks. I'm sure you'll earn whatever Sam has paid you."

Now I know his name, Sam ... rhymes with Spam.

"No way," says Sam. "This may be a gift for you, but I paid for it. I'm going to enjoy it, even if I don't get the ladder view."

Men can be so adolescent. I blink a few times to keep from rolling my eyes. That would be unprofessional. "Part of the contract is that you get a photo of me in my get-up. The boss doesn't like it when we don't come back with a photo. He says his photo album is a great marketing tool." Oh, geez, it sounds like I'm describing a pimp.

"He sounds obnoxious," Jake says.

"Heavens, no, he's not. Rex is a sweetheart." Now it sounds like he's my boyfriend. I'm batting zero. I need a moment alone. "I'll just slip into the bathroom and change. Since Sam's lobbied for the bikini ... " It's just as well since I paid thirty dollars for a wax yesterday. I ease past Jake and head for the bathroom. When I close the door, the mirrors are still fogged and the scent of sandalwood wafts from the shower. I close my eyes and breathe in the spicy scent, imagining Jake's hands all over my body, soaping from my quadriceps up. My hands creep to my breasts. I pretend my hands are his ... and pinch my nipples. Oh, geez, I could go a long way with this. What if Jake were to slip into the bathroom right about now? He'd wrap an arm around my waist and ease me forward over the vanity. His thick rod would press against my back. He'd sort of roll it around my butt, and that's when I'd take the not so subtle hint and bend deeper over the counter. He'd slip a hand between my legs and find my bud, which by this time would be throbbing. Oh, great Scot, the juices are starting to flow. Maybe I can just rub my legs together for a few minutes and ...

Earth to Amy! This is so *not* like me. I don't believe in instant attraction, at least, not until now. I press my thumbs into my eye sockets, pressure points for a reality check. My brain fart must be due to lack of sleep and too many anatomical charts. I remind myself of the no fraternizing rule, which if I recall, is number nine in the Fantasy Maid Manual. Besides, this guy's engaged. As I pull my t-shirt over my head and unzip my jeans, I think back to my previous job as a theme park hotel maid. No costumes, but the hours didn't work with school and the money barely covered the cost of gas to get there. Yep, this job has made all the difference in paying for my education. I don't know how else I could have realized my dream.

By the time I've positioned the bottom triangle of my bikini and made sure the top provides as much coverage as a few inches of spandex allow, I fluff my bangs and salute my mirror image. I'm tingling all over. I'm usually a bit jittery at this point in the gig anyway. The unveiling (that would be me in costume) and the subsequent client reaction can be unnerving. But today I'm beyond nerves. I take a few cleansing breaths. As the manual emphasizes, "Be sexy and be strong."

In the mood for more Crimson Romance?
Check out *Falling Again by Peggy Bird* at *CrimsonRomance.com*.